Weeds

A Story in Seven Chapters

by

Jerome K. Jerome

edited with an introduction and notes
by Carolyn W. de la L. Oulton

Victorian Secrets 2012

Published by

Victorian Secrets Limited
32 Hanover Terrace
Brighton BN2 9SN

www.victoriansecrets.co.uk

Weeds: A Story in Seven Chapters by Jerome K. Jerome
First published in 1892
This Victorian Secrets edition 2012

Introduction and notes © 2012 by Carolyn W. de la L. Oulton
This edition © 2012 by Victorian Secrets
Composition and design by Catherine Pope
Cover image © iStockPhoto/coloroftime

A catalogue record for this book is available from the British Library.

ISBN 978-1-906469-40-5

CONTENTS

INTRODUCTION

A brief biography of Jerome K. Jerome

The almost tastelessly famous Jerome K. Jerome, like his friend J. M. Barrie (a prolific author whose creation of Peter Pan continues to eclipse his other work), was in one sense always a victim of his own success. The author of eight novels (as well as fifteen collections of sketches and short stories, two autobiographical works, at least one attributed book on stage conventions, over thirty plays and a substantial body of journalism), he is remembered almost exclusively for one youthful *jeu d'esprit*, the best-selling *Three Men in a Boat* of 1889. That is by readers who even recognise the source of the much loved quote 'I like work. It fascinates me. I could sit and look at it for hours.' Abused in the press during his lifetime as a 'New Humourist', well into his middle years Jerome struggled to convince reviewers that he was capable of serious, mature work. Of the novel that made him famous he claimed in the year before he died that 'I did not intend to write a funny book, at first. I did not know I was a humourist. I have never been sure about it' (*My Life and Times*, 74-75).

Few readers would agree with his self-appraisal, but certainly there was nothing in the hardships of Jerome's early life in London to inspire comedy; he once noted bitterly, 'There have been a good many funny things said and written about hardupishness, but the reality is not funny, for all that. ... No, there is nothing at all funny in poverty – to the poor' ('On being hard up', 14). In theory this was a subject he should have known nothing about at first hand. Born on 2 May 1859 in an imposing house in Walsall, Staffordshire, Jerome was the fourth child and second son of a non-conformist preacher and businessman and his wife Marguerite (née Jones). The family had moved from Appledore in Devonshire a few years earlier, changing their surname on arrival from Clapp to Jerome. Quite why a man who thereby landed himself with the name Jerome Jerome would want to confuse matters further by bestowing the same name on his younger son remains unclear. The Clapp resurfaced in his son's middle name, but Jerome Clapp Jerome the younger had reinvented himself by 1880 as the more glamorous Jerome Klapka Jerome, and always published under the name by which he is commonly known, Jerome K. Jerome.

By 1860 Jerome senior's heavy investment in coal mining had failed, leaving the family without a source of steady income. In 1861 he relocated to Poplar in the East End of London, where he put most of the remaining capital into an ironmongery in Limehouse, sending home as much as he could afford to his wife and children while living on subsistence rates himself. Marguerite took the children to live in a more modest house in Stourbridge, and it was here that their elder son Milton died of croup in January 1862. By the end of the year the remaining family members were all living together in Poplar, in a small house in 'one of those lifeless streets, made of two drab walls upon which the level lines, formed by the precisely even window-sills and doorsteps, stretch in weary perspective from end to end, suggesting petrified diagrams proving dead problems' (*Paul Kelver*, 1). Here the street boys would torment the child Jerome as an obvious outsider, and his mother would console him by saying that it was because he was a gentleman. Less helpfully as it turned out, his parents also took him to hear the premillenarian Dr Cummings preach on the imminent end of the world. Not surprisingly by the time he reached his teens he was already being plagued by religious doubts.

The house in Sussex Street, Poplar was the first home Jerome could properly remember and all his life he remained fascinated by the district, later claiming, 'about the East End of London there is a menace, a haunting terror that is to be found nowhere else. The awful silence of its weary streets. The ashen faces, with their lifeless eyes that rise out of the shadow and are lost. It was these surroundings in which my childhood was passed that gave to me, I suppose, my melancholy, brooding disposition' (*My Life and Times*, 11). Despite a series of forays into new schemes, including a projected railway line, the Jeromes were never again able to sustain a secure middle-class lifestyle, and only managed to send their remaining son to school for four years, between the ages of ten and fourteen, after which he left for his first job as a clerk at the London and North-Western Railway.

By this time his father had died (in 1871), one of his sisters (Paulina) had married and the other (Blandina) was working away from home as a governess. When Marguerite Jerome died in 1875 the sixteen-year-old Jerome was forced to fend for himself, moving from one cheap lodging to another before throwing up his job in 1878 for a brief career as an itinerant actor, an experience that is vividly described in his first book *On the Stage – and Off: the brief career of a would-be actor* (1885). After two years travelling the country with a series of low budget companies, he was sleeping rough on the London streets when he was rescued, apparently through a chance encounter with an old friend who had also fallen on hard times. Through this friend's good auspices Jerome embarked on a new career as a penny-a-line journalist, a period of his life he would remember with some enthusiasm despite the poor pay and insecure prospects. Next came a brief stint as a school teacher, but this by his own account was not a great success. By 1881 he was working as a solicitor's clerk on the Strand, where he remained until a year after the runaway success of *Three Men in a Boat*, written shortly after his marriage in 1888 to Georgina (Ettie) Marris, the recently divorced wife of his first cousin.

The instant popular success of this comic account of Jerome's boating holidays, many of them with his erstwhile fellow lodger George Wingrave (George) and Carl Hentschel (Harris) set the tone for reviews up till and even beyond the end of his life. Most refused to take him seriously, and for the more élite journals, his deliberate and unapologetic use of lower-middle-class slang made him an easy target. In fact as Jonathan Wild points out, the Three Men casually proffer tips and take cabs despite what is presumably their relatively low income, in a manner that suggests an 'aspirational' target audience wanting to read about a lifestyle just above their own rather than about their own shared experiences (67). Wild rightly emphasises that 'J' more than once alludes to ''Arrys and 'Arriets' in order to distance his characters from this stereotype of the cockney holidaymaker on the rampage. Nonetheless, reviewers persisted in referring to Jerome as the embodiment of an ''Arry', even referring to him as ''Arry K. 'Arry' and then, as he bitterly remembered, they would 'solemnly lecture me on the sin of mistaking vulgarity for humour and impertinence for wit' (*My Life and Times* 52). Of all the journals it was the influential *Punch* which he felt had done most to perpetuate this image of his writing as vulgar and ephemeral. It was in vain for him to protest:

> Whenever the superior book-reviewer, sampling a new work of mine, has expended on me all his stock epithets of cad, boor, blackguard, snob, liar, brute, bank-clerk, new humourist, thief, upstart, and suchlike subtle thrusts characteristic of the new criticism, he invariably concludes his "notice" by calling me a "Cockney." The main portion of this abuse I have by long practice schooled myself to bear with equanimity. I even endeavour to derive from it some benefit, as one should from all criticism. But the "bank-clerk" and the "Cockney" do, I confess, rankle within my breast. I have never been a bank-clerk. I have served as clerk in most other offices, but never in a bank. To call me "Cockney" is even more unjust. Meaning from the beginning to be a writer, I took the precaution of selecting my birthplace in a dismal town in the centre of the Staffordshire coalfields, a hundred and fifty miles, at least, away from London' ('The Idlers' Club', *The Idler* vol 4 (August 1893 - January 1894), p.108).

But while he was routinely forced to defend his ambivalent status as the most famous of the 'New Humourists', it was always Jerome's ambition to become known as a serious writer. Despite his new responsibilities as a family man (Ettie already had a daughter, Elsie, by her first marriage and Rowena was born in 1889), he made valiant if futile efforts to avoid writing simply as 'the author of *Three Men in a Boat*'. His fictional counterpart Paul Kelver, in the 1902 book of the same name, suffers from a long-standing desire to write tragically moving fiction and an ineluctable propensity for comic anecdote. Jerome was desperate to avoid this fate. Despite his best efforts however he was haunted all his life by the label of 'New Humourist'.

From 1895 Jerome leased a substantial house in Ewelme, Oxfordshire, and it was here that two locals were heard arguing over what precisely he was famous *for*. One man thought that he wrote books, but was promptly snubbed with, 'He rowed three men in a boat, and then won the race; that's what he's noted for' ('Three Men in a Boat', 5). Notwithstanding his abiding fascination with the city, Jerome spent most of his time in Oxfordshire from the turn of the century, first in Ewelme and from 1909 in Marlow. In 1902 he published one of his most serious works to date, the semi-autobiographical *Paul Kelver*, which was gratifyingly compared by a series of critics to his favourite Dickens novel, *David Copperfield*.

Following the outbreak of war in 1914 Jerome was at first an enthusiastic propagandist, and contrived to join a French ambulance unit in 1916. Six months later he came back from the front 'cured of any sneaking regard I may ever have had for war' (*My Life and Times* 205) and his 1919 novel *All Roads Lead to Calvary* notably demonises a crowd who lynch a young conscientious objector. The socialist novel *Anthony John* followed in 1921. But despite his attempts to redefine himself as a writer of political fiction, Jerome was still forced to warn a correspondent in 1925 that he would be happy to address an assembly on literary topics 'Presuming that you and your friends, will be willing to let me talk, perhaps, on serious subjects' (to Henry McClelland, 9 September 1925). *My Life and Times*, a vivid if somewhat unreliable autobiography published in 1926, shows Jerome still struggling with the label 'humourist' nearly forty years after *Three Men in a Boat*. As if to prove his point, his obituary in *The Times* in 1927 described him as 'a typical humourist of the eighties' (*The Times*, 15 June 1927, 18) Just over forty years later an astonishing revelation added one more to the impressive list of Jeromian outputs, although it would take yet another four decades (the apparent neatness of these forty-year interludes might well have pleased the tidy-minded Jerome) before the significance of this find could be properly understood.

Weeds

The following commentary reveals important aspects of the plot. Readers new to the novel might wish to treat the Introduction as an afterword.

It was a letter to his publisher J. W. Arrowsmith, auctioned at Sotheby's in 1968, which first revealed that the 'K Mc K' on the title page of an unknown (and possibly unpublished) novella called *Weeds* was none other than the world famous Jerome K. Jerome. More puzzling still, *Weeds* dated from 1892, meaning that he had missed an obvious chance to cash in on his name just three years after *Three Men in a Boat*. Available (as far as is known) only in the copyright libraries, this obscure title was intended to be part of the Arrowsmith Notebook series, printed on one side of the paper only, and with the spine at the top. The mystery of its anonymous authorship and Arrowsmith's evident reluctance to release it for general sale lie in a series of letters from Jerome to Arrowsmith written in the autumn of 1892.

That September he wrote urging his publisher to go ahead with the book, which he had taken such trouble with not for the sake of any emolument but in hopes of gaining a reputation. The controlled desperation is obvious as he alternately urges and reassures, 'If I weaken my resolve the object of all my labour is gone ... I don't think the public who would be offended will read beyond the first few pages. The thing will not interest them. The thoughtful public will not be offended' Certainly there is nothing in the final copy of the book, in which a young man is seen by his wife evidently kissing her cousin, to give undue offence to the most prudish reader. But as the letters reveal, this vital scene is a heavily coded representation of illicit sex. Jerome goes on, 'I read it to my wife and she never guessed the drift of it' and suggests that Arrowsmith should try a similar experiment on his own wife, 'she will gather the idea that they are only kissing each other. The phrase "They are alone with Heaven" will only convey itself to a very limited public indeed, to that public I am writing for. The general reader will never care for the book. You see in this I am not the business man I am the artist. The whole attempt is artistic' (letter to J. W. Arrowsmith [1892]). Clearly Arrowsmith was not convinced and the next letter suggests that the book should go out without the publisher's name, or for that matter his own, 'I wd put my name to it after it had passed through the critics [sic] hands. But if my name was on a serious work like this it would never get fair treatment. They would all say I had tried to be funny and failed.' In a postscript he offers to substitute 'The room dissolves and fades. They are alone with Nature' for 'Their quivering limbs entwine' (undated letter to J. W. Arrowsmith). This change was adopted and the last letter on the subject contains an anxious, 'How does Weeds move? Do you think it would be useful in a month or so to let it leak out that it is mine? About how long does it take for a book by an unknown name to attract any attention?' (undated letter to J. W. Arrowsmith). The lack of extant copies suggests that Arrowsmith had either gone through the motions of copyrighting the book on Jerome's behalf without issuing even a limited edition, or more likely lost his nerve at the last minute and cancelled or at least greatly reduced the print run.

No further correspondence has come to light in connection with this incident, but the novella itself is significant not least because it *was* written by the author of *Three Men in a Boat*. In the comic novel that made him famous Jerome pictures young men ostensibly working in banks but actually spending most of their time in homosocial bonding and ludicrous escapades involving rerouted trains, recalcitrant boats and tinned pineapple chunks. Three years later *Weeds* uses a comparable figure, the junior partner in an indigo importing firm, Dick Selwyn, to disrupt just such a picture of carefree and innocent youth. Jerome had originally implied to Arrowsmith in 1889 that *Three Men in a Boat* was something like F. Anstey's *Vice Versâ* (which the firm had recently published in 1882), and it is possible that Dick is named for Anstey's comically subversive schoolboy-turned-merchant Dick Bultitude. Located in the suburbs, *Weeds* might also be expected to reference George and Weedon Grossmith's famous *Diary of a Nobody* (1888-89).

Certainly the narrator does satirise the life of the suburban middle class, as he had done in *Three Men in a Boat* in a sarcastic (but uncannily prescient) commentary on the furnishings of lower-middle-class dwellings:

> Will rows of our willow-pattern dinner-plates be ranged above the chimneypieces of the great in the years 2000 and odd? … The "sampler" that the eldest daughter did at school will be spoken of as "tapestry of the Victorian era," and be almost priceless. The blue-and-white mugs of the present-day roadside inn will be hunted up, all cracked and chipped, and sold for their weight in gold, and rich people will use them for claret cups; and travellers from Japan will buy up all the "Presents from Ramsgate," and "Souvenirs of Margate," that may have escaped destruction, and take them back to Jedo as ancient English curios. (45-46)

Weeds gently pokes fun at Dick's aspirations, as he:

> sees the small semi-detached villa which is the present abode of the Selwyn household, give place to a real villa; a villa boldly standing up by itself, needing no support from other villas—a dignified villa, preferring to keep other villas at a certain distance, objecting to familiarity and crowding. A fair-sized garden, which a fond proprietor might, without unreason, allude to as "grounds," encircles the house; and in this garden there are greenhouses, through which a City man on Sunday afternoons might take the City friends who have come down to see his "little place," casually mentioning the while, as a joke against himself, the amount each bunch of grapes or orchid blossom growing there has cost him.

> He almost thinks he sees a neat two-horsed brougham waiting

before the door. Why should he not? Two-horsed broughams are by
no means unknown to the indigo trade. (p. 35)

Jerome enjoys several affectionate digs at a stolidly respectable class
who nonetheless aspire to the ostentatious displays of aestheticism.
The Selwyns live in a house called 'Acacia Villa' and the narrator notes
with some amusement that the 154 identical houses in the road are
equally determined to be 'artistic' and 'There is much coloured glass
about the doors and windows. There are many white-railed balconies—
none of them of the slightest possible use, except perhaps to afford
compensation to the cats for the almost entire lack of any roof space
practicable for business.' (p. 40).

But despite this banter with the reader, the chapter headings make
it very clear that the book has a serious moral message. In an obvious
allusion to the Genesis story of Adam and Eve, the story is divided
into seven parts:

> I. THE GARDEN
> II. OF THE WEEDS IN THE GARDEN
> III. THE WEEDS GROW
> IV. THE VIGILANCE OF THE HUSBANDMAN
> V. THE NEGLIGENCE OF THE HUSBANDMAN
> VI. THE STRANGLING OF THE FLOWERS
> VII. IN THE WILDERNESS

While Jerome by this stage of his life had largely abandoned
orthodox Christianity, he made deliberate use of Old Testament
teaching to present a story of betrayal in apocalyptic terms. Far from
being an unimportant aberration by a naturally comic writer, *Weeds*
raises intriguing questions about Jerome's views on illicit sexuality,
degeneration and the human potential for evil. In taking the suburban
villa as a type of the Garden of Eden he plays on clichés about young
married love, but also reminds his readers that in the biblical story the
archetypal married lovers bring evil into the world in succumbing to

temptation. Reworking the familiar treatment of the city commuter as harmlessly affected, Jerome brings the power of evil to the suburban villa with much the same intent as writers such as Wilkie Collins and Mary Braddon, and more recently his friend Sir Arthur Conan Doyle, had invested the serene country house with menace. Like Robert Louis Stevenson's 1886 *Jekyll and Hyde*, *Weeds* exploits the divided spaces of the city as a symbol of inner corruption, variously charting the movements of the middle-class Dick across ambiguous spaces such as theatres and horse drawn cabs, and the ostensibly pure domain of the suburban home. Like Jekyll, Dick is a sympathetic figure troubled by vicious impulses he attempts unsuccessfully to disavow or quarantine from his better self.

In its treatment of sexual deviance as a sign of degeneration rather than a source of plot tension or social protest, *Weeds* is very much of its time. Jonathan Dollimore notes that Max Nordau's *Degeneration*,[1] first published in English in 1895, depends precisely on a fluid relationship between good and evil, the theme fictionalised by Jerome three years earlier. Dollimore argues that 'For all its 560-odd pages of unflaggingly confident denunciation of the degenerate, and its equally confident affirmation of the truly, self-evidently, civilized, this is a book written in the knowledge that the two are in a terrifying proximity and are often indistinguishable' (103). Tellingly, Andrew Smith notes that the ease with which French theories of degeneration dating back to mid-century were transferred to the popular realm 'suggests that the theory was always, in essence, a cultural narrative' (15).

Jerome could have read *Degeneration* in the original German in 1892, although his first known reference to it is in connection with the English translation in 1895, when he described it in an editorial in his journal *To-day* as 'suggestive, audacious, interesting, showing that width of range which is so fatal in science and so desirable everywhere else' (6 April 1895, 274). In a carefully sustained criticism of the book, Jerome points out that parallels between particular groups do not in

---

1   See Appendix A on p. 79

themselves prove connections. Incidentally his response is not least interesting for his own characteristic assumption that the aesthetic influence he had enthusiastically satirised in *Weeds* had already petered out by 1892. This habit of alternately ridiculing and denying threatening social trends is typical of Jerome's 1890s journalism. For all its gentle mockery of painted glass and faux antiques, he would not necessarily have acknowledged that *Weeds* itself links aestheticism to degeneration. But as Jenny Bourne Taylor argues, 'The discourse of degeneration undoubtedly pervaded biological, psychological and social theory during the late nineteenth century' partly because 'It ... enabled connections to be made between apparently very different forms and processes. Its power and popularity lay precisely in its vagueness – its ability to be pressed into the service of very different social and political agendas.' (16) As William Greenslade explains, degeneration theory was important not least because it established 'necessary boundaries' between the normal and the deviant (18).

Jerome's account of Dick's evil impulses is deliberately more threatening than H. G. Wells's 1891 analogy of the professional classes and the 'passive receptivity to what chance and the water bring along' (Wells 8) of the ascidian. According to Wells, 'Every respectable citizen of the professional classes passes through a period of activity and imagination. ... He shocks his aunts. Presently, however, he realizes the sober aspect of things. He becomes dull; he enters a profession; suckers appear on his head; and he studies. Finally, by virtue of these he settles down – he marries.' (9) Meanwhile Nordau's treatise famously invokes the role of the philistine middle class as an antidote to decadence. In *Three Men in a Boat* Jerome had indeed celebrated what Lyn Hapgood terms 'the intrinsic value of the ordinary' (36) but in the later account it is this very middle class which proves the locus of evil, precisely because it is so hard to detect.

Smith suggests a complex picture dating back to the mid-century when Samuel Smiles and Charles Kingsley 'both constructed a model of a divided male subject, one who asserts a social role in order to overcome a distracting biological presence' (4). This imperative is repeatedly associated with Dick, who is tormented by his own illicit desires long before becoming attracted to Jessie. At one point he specifically asks himself whether Daisy would still 'love him if she knew *all* his life. Would her deep, clear eyes look up to his, as they do now, if they could see into his heart—if they could see the evil thoughts that writhe and twine about each other there—the foolish, evil thoughts that, let in youth to run too often in and out, have come, at last, to make the place their home, and will not be forbidden?' (p. 39) Just such questions would become the acknowledged province of Sarah Grand, whose *The Heavenly Twins* of 1893 raised disturbing questions about the relationship between moral restraint and eugenic fitness to contribute to the next generation. Significantly at this point Dick is tortured not by anything he has actually done, but by immoral thoughts which long indulgence has now rendered impossible to control. His diseased mind is specifically linked to popular theories of degeneration, as the narrator warns, 'a man's heart is the link between the animalism from which we have sprung and the spiritualism towards which we tend. Let it suffice that we keep our outsides clean; that we watch ever, lest in some weak, fevered moment one of these same small evil thoughts creep out and, reaching the light, become an evil deed, immortal like ourselves' (p. 39). Disturbingly, these animalistic instincts are both deeply ingrained and natural. Jerome would continue to stress this point in his fiction and journalism.

There may possibly be an echo of Vernon Lee's 1887 ghost story 'Amour Dure' in 'The Woman of the Saeter'; first published in *The Idler* in 1893, the inset story is told through the letters of a traveller in Norway who becomes possessed by the ghost of a femme fatale. In a series of letters to a friend he recounts his descent into obsession, and how in social isolation 'The culture of the centuries has fallen from me as a flimsy garment whirled away by the mountain wind, the old savage instincts of the race lie bare' (65). Describing the 'caterpillar' metamorphosis of the girl as she becomes a woman, the narrator of

Weeds comments, 'in a day, the chill spring of youth gives place to the summer of womanhood; and lo! before our dazzled eyes there dances, laughing, a glorious creature of the sun. And our first *natural* instinct is to follow it, cap in hand, seeking to possess it, so that we may destroy it' (p. 42, emphasis added). Jessie herself, who has been transformed from an ungainly adolescent 'who never understood when she was not wanted' (p. 26) into a pre-Raphaelite stunner with auburn hair and pale skin, seems initially set to play the role of femme fatale when she comes to visit her cousin Daisy. But as the narrative progresses it becomes clear that she is no more suited to this role than to the equally transgressive status of the emerging New Woman. In an incisive exploration of *fin-de-siècle* representations of the sexual woman, Jennifer Hedgecock argues that, 'While both the femme fatale and the New Woman act on their own principles, their intentions on this point are very different. Each has an agenda, and the primary concern of the New Woman is to integrate her values into mainstream culture, while the femme fatale is a kind of receptacle, internalizing the values and beliefs of society and accepting this consensus in order to render her scheming successful.' (194)

Jessie's naive responsiveness to Dick is anything but scheming, as the narrator makes clear, 'She has awakened one morning to find, as by some magic that she herself as yet can hardly understand, her whole world—or, at all events, the (to her) more interesting portion of it—at her feet. Without her even stretching out her arm to grasp it, the sceptre of authority, that men will fret their lives out to obtain possession of for a few troubled hours, has been placed within her hand' (p. 44). Michael Mason has argued that from mid-century onwards sexual signs actually became harder to decode as parasexuality became more acceptable, and *Weeds* carefully charts Jessie's artless descent from affectionate teasing to flirtation and suggestiveness while obfuscating the precise moment at which she realises she is acting disloyally to Daisy. Jerome was always outraged by the kind of prudishness that denied sex education to young women, writing to a female reader in the Correspondence section of *To-day* in 1897, 'It is to me ununderstandable that society should encourage a conspiracy of silence in this matter. The subject is one that you ought to be able to discuss frankly and freely with your mother, or with some older married woman friend of sympathy and sense; but I have no doubt you would be met with horrified indignation, as though the whole scheme of the Creator were some highly indelicate piece of business that He ought to have been ashamed of Himself for working out.' (12 June 1897)

It is significant that Daisy forgives Jessie her part in the break-up of her marriage, before leaving Dick. In doing so she reminds him that while 'it will be a very difficult position for both of us' it will be 'more so for me than for you' (p. 77). This final sympathy with the innocent woman who will be victimised by conventional society, and likewise with the treacherous cousin who must now either marry a suitor without love, or risk exposure, brings Jerome as close as he would ever get to the territory of New Woman writing. Intriguingly the lack of attribution on the title cover might indeed lead readers to assume a female author. Taken with the long hidden letters to Arrowsmith, this free-floating authorship of a virtually unknown work raises all sorts of questions about the late Victorian treatment of sexuality and how it is codified for the 'one in a hundred' who can interpret the signs correctly.

BIBLIOGRAPHY

Dollimore, Jonathan. 'Perversion, Degeneration and the Death Drive' in *Sexualities in Victorian Britain*. Ed Andrew H. Miller and James Eli Adams. Bloomington and Indianapolis: Indiana University Press 1996. 96-117.

Greenslade, William P. *Degeneration, Culture and the Novel: 1880-1940*. Cambridge: Cambridge University Press 2010.

Hapgood, Lyn. *Margins of desire: the suburbs in fiction and culture, 1880-1925*. Manchester: Manchester University Press 2009.

Hedgecock, Jennifer. *The Femme Fatale in Victorian Literature: the Danger and the Threat*. New York: Cambria Press 2008.

Jerome K. Jerome. *My Life and Times*. London: Folio Society 1992.

--'On being hard up' in *Idle Thoughts of an Idle Fellow*, pp. 11-19.

--*On the Stage – and Off: the brief career of a would-be actor*. Stroud: Sutton 1991.

--*Paul Kelver*. London: Hutchinson and Co. 1902.

--*The Other Jerome*. Ed Martin Green. Nonesuch 2008.

--*To-day*. Editorial. 6 April 1895. 273-75.

--*To-day*, Correspondence. 12 June 1897. 206.

--*Three Men in a Boat*. Oxford: Oxford University Press 1998.

-- Jerome K. Jerome to Henry McClelland, 9 September 1925, MS.152/53/3, Mitchell Library, Glasgow.

Mason, Michael. *The Making of Victorian Sexuality*. Oxford: Oxford University Press 1994.

Smith, Andrew. *Victorian Demons: Medicine, Masculinity and the Gothic at the Fin-de-Siècle*. Manchester: MUP 2008.

Taylor, Jenny Bourne. 'Psychology at the *Fin de Siècle*' in Gail Marshall, ed. *The Cambridge Guide to the Fin de Siècle*. Cambridge: Cambridge University Press 2007. 13-30.

'Three Men in a Boat'. *Oxford Chronicle and Berks and Bucks Gazette*. 25 September 1897. 5.

The Times. Obituaries. 'Mr Jerome K. Jerome'. 15 June 1927. 18.

Wells, H. G. '*Zoological Retrogression*' in *The Fin de Siècle: a Reader in Cultural History c. 1890-1900*. Ed Sally Ledger and Roger Luckhurst. Oxford: Oxford University Press 2000. First published 1891.

Wild, Jonathan. *The Rise of the Office Clerk in Literary Culture, 1880-1939*. Basingstoke: Palgrave Macmillan 2006.

A NOTE ON THE TEXT

The text is taken from the first (and only), limited edition produced by Arrowsmith in 1892. Obvious printing errors have been silently corrected.

ABOUT THE EDITOR

Carolyn Oulton is a Reader in Victorian Literature and Co-Director of the International Centre for Victorian Women Writers at Canterbury Christ Church University. Her first biography was *Let the Flowers Go: A Life of Mary Cholmondeley* (Pickering and Chatto 2009) and her biography *Below the Fairy City: A Life of Jerome K. Jerome* is published by Victorian Secrets.

Weeds: A Story in Seven Chapters

CHAPTER ONE

The Garden

"Oh! Oh, how delightful! Oh, I am so glad!"

And two exceedingly pretty dimpled hands, one of which holds the letter that their owner is reading, meet and ecstatically clasp each other as if pretending, after the sycophantic manner of dependents, that they also are delighted.

"What's delightful? What are you glad about?" asked Dick Selwyn, joint proprietor of those same dimpled hands, laying down the newspaper from which he, in common with the rest of the British public on this morning, has been regaling himself with the latest "amusing divorce case"[1] (amusing, that is, to all except the insignificant minority personally concerned, to whom, maybe, the whole affair appears rather as a tragedy—just commenced), and insinuatingly pushing his empty cup in the direction of the coffeepot.

"Why, Jessie is up in London, and is coming on to us to-day!" answers Daisy, keeping her eyes still fixed upon her letter, and pouring out Dick's coffee at the same time—a feat in domestic gymnastics the like of which young housewives are curiously fond of performing, and the watching of which never fails to excite amazement and alarm in the bosom of the male audience.

Dick waits while one white hand, left to rely entirely on its own gumption, flutters doubtfully, like a little blind bird, above the breakfast

---

1 Before the Matrimonial Causes Act of 1857 only the very wealthy could afford to divorce, by a special Act of Parliament. The Married Women's Property Acts of 1870 and 1882 allowed women to keep their earnings after marriage, making it easier for them to seek divorce. Jerome may be referring to the scandalous O'Shea divorce case of 1890.

things. At last, guided by some subtle sense of its own, it lights upon and helps him to sugar and milk; and he, marvelling much, draws his cup towards him.

"Who's Jessie?"

"Oh, Dick!" (in a tone of surprised indignation) "you know Jessie— Jessie Craig?"

"Oh that! Is she going to stop?"

Dick has recollections of a shy, gawky girl, a member of that unblessed body of, comparatively useless, individuals upon which the average man bestows contemptuously the bitter epithet of "my wife's relations"—a stupid girl from whom he and Daisy, in their sweethearting days, seemed never able to escape, who never understood when she was not wanted (which was frequently), or, if she did understand, never knew how to act. He does not look forward to her threatened visit with any very pleasurable anticipations.

"I'll telegraph and put her off, if you object to her coming, Dick," says his wife, laying down the letter, and speaking in a voice as near that of anger as the sweet, firm mouth can form. "I thought you liked Jessie?"

"Oh, yes, I like her well enough," replies Dick, recollectful of many hypocritical overtures of friendship made to that young lady at a period when it was his policy to ingratiate himself with every one who could whisper a word or a bark or a chirp for or against him into Daisy's ear. "Let her come by all means. I was merely wondering what we should do with her."

"Don't talk about the poor girl as if she were a new piece of furniture. Oh, Dick, you are so silly this morning!" and Mrs. Selwyn laughs.

It is a very wonderful laugh, Daisy Selwyn's. It is quiet and low, and yet, in theatres and places where they laugh, you can generally hear it above all other laughs.

It is a born leader of laughs. It draws forth laughs from dry old throats where they have lain hidden for years, no one, and especially not their harbourer's, suspecting even their existence. It musters other laughs around it, and heads them against gathering forces of sulkiness and ill-temper. At the first note of its music cross old folks turn away to smile, and demon babies, who are trying to annoy their parents by screaming themselves to death, stop to gurgle, and become, indeed, quite reformed characters, for about ten minutes.

"Well, you know what I mean," replies Dick, joining in the laugh. "She's quite a child."

"A —." Daisy checks the exclamation on her lips, and instead says: "You haven't seen Jessie since we were married, have you?"

"No, I don't think I have," is Dick's careless answer. "Saw enough of her before," he adds, but not aloud.

"Do you know how long we have been married, Dick?"

Dick pushes away his plate, and looks across the table at his wife.

Dick Selwyn is of that average type of Englishman who, if their real feelings were to be estimated by their own expression of them, might be held to possess none at all. His regard for Daisy, to all outward seeming, is that of the common or villa husband[2] for the lady who superintends his household; but beneath the unpromising surface there lies hidden a deep well of tenderness for this sweet blossom from the tree of womanhood that he has plucked to wear upon his breast. His love for her has strengthened, not weakened, since the day it first came to him. How well he remembers that sunny afternoon! She is standing, dressed in her favourite white, knee-deep amid the tall grass of the old Kentish orchard, one rounded arm stretched out to reach a tempting apple that just eludes her grasp. He helps her to pluck the fruit, and they eat it together, laughing. The first few bites are very sweet, but there is a worm at the core; so she throws it away, and it lies on the ground rotting.[3]

2   The allusion to 'common or garden' butterfly or flower both echoes the central theme of the Garden of Eden and reminds the reader of Dick's ordinariness as a dweller in the suburbs.

3   The tree of knowledge of good and evil described in Genesis is traditionally presented as an apple tree. Here the apple is symbolic of an impure love that will ultimately be rejected by the woman.

And this morning, as Dick looks across the breakfast table, he sees the same Daisy he saw then. The green of the orchard has given place to a yellow wallpaper, adorned with a few cheap engravings, an uncompromisingly modern-looking "early English" sideboard, and a cheery fire, crackling beneath a "Queen Anne" overmantel.[4] But beyond this rearrangement of the back-ground, the picture remains unaltered. There is still the simple white frock—it is Daisy's one extravagance, the wearing of white frocks, for which her conscience never fails to prick her the moment she sits down to check the week's washing bill—still the same sunny, restful face; still the same trustful, clear grey eyes.

Marriage is too often a witch's cauldron, transforming a winsome sweetheart into a crabbed wife. Sometimes, but less frequently, it is as the sword with which the mermaid pierced her heart, creating out of the soulless foam of the sea a woman.[5] But Daisy has passed unchanged through the searching flames that burn upon Hymen's[6] altar. The microscope of married life has revealed to Dick no fresh beauty, no hidden flaw in her nature: the metal was too true to be moulded or marred by the hammers of circumstance.

Her question has recalled to him the sweet full days that they have shared together, the brightness and content that she has brought into his life, and a flood of loving words with which to answer her wells up into his heart. Not possessing, however, the mental pumping machinery necessary for raising them to his lips, he only says, smiling:

"It doesn't seem very long."

"Three years, Dick!"

He crosses and, bending over her, softly kisses the smooth brown hair.

"Do you know, Daisy, at one time, in the early days, just after we were

4   A shelf or decorative woodwork hung over the fire mantel.

5   An allusion to Christian Hans Anderson's popular story of 'The Little Mermaid' (1836).

6   The Greek god of weddings.

married, I used to get quite frightened, thinking of the years before us. I used to wonder if we should ever come to be like other married people, like the people one sees around one everywhere—always quarrelling and bitter about one thing or another, not caring for each other any more."

"Oh, Dick, what a dreadful thing to think!"

"Yes, wasn't it? And then, as the days went by, and we seemed to grow closer and closer to one another, and you got to be more and more to me, then I used to get frightened for myself. I used to wonder if you would ever be disappointed with me—find out that I was not quite all that you had thought me."

"But how could I, Dick? I knew you so well."

"Are you sure you did?"

A puzzled look comes into Daisy's eyes.

"Of course, you foolish fellow! Why do you ask so seriously?"

"Did I?" Dick laughs. "I feel serious, I suppose, when I think of anything making you cease to care for me."

"And how do you know that I haven't ceased to care for you, Mr. Conceited?" answers Daisy saucily.

"Well, you hadn't last week," retorts Dick, pinching her ear. "You stated—quite unsolicited, too—that I was a 'dear, dear fellow' —two 'dears' and that you did love me, *so* much, with a strong accent on the 'so.'"

"Oh, Dick! when did I say that?"

Daisy seems somewhat sceptical. Such emphatic expositions of emotion are not customary with her.

In those hushed aisles, sacred to sentiment, where men do not care to speak what they think, women, more devout, deem it almost sacrilege to think what they feel. When Dick, leaning against the pigstye wall —of all places in the world for a proposal—had suddenly felt himself compelled, he knew not why, to abruptly interrupt a discussion on the culture of tomatoes with the utterly inconsequent inquiry: "Daisy, will you be my wife?" Daisy, keeping her eyes fixed the while on an elderly porker who, clearly regarding himself as Dick's rival, sat encouraging her with an affectionate leer, had, after a pause, simply answered: "Yes, Dick;" and had then laughed at him for his choice of time and place: and when Dick, her other admirer having been left to muse upon the misunderstandableness of womankind, and to smother his disappointment in potato peelings, had, stopping with his hand upon the garden door and endeavouring to assume the tone of a man eager for information, asked what he then knew to be the totally unnecessary question: "Do you love me, Daisy?" she had answered as before:

"Yes, Dick."

And now, after three years of blameless married life, she stands accused of having voluntarily and shamelessly avowed her love for him, and that with an amount of compressed gush she should not have considered herself capable of. She naturally looks for an explanation.

"Oh, you hadn't all your senses about you when you said it, I grant you," acknowledges Dick, laughing. "It was the night you went to bed early with a headache; and when I came in, you were talking in your sleep. I think you must have been arguing with somebody about it, because you were so very emphatic. You said: 'Yes, yes, I do! He is a dear, dear fellow, and I do love him—*so* much!' At least, I took it that the statement had reference to me."

"Yes, I suppose it must have," replies Daisy, ruefully. "Oh, dear! I thought I'd got over all that."

Daisy refers not to her love for Dick, as might seem to be implied, but to the habit of talking in her sleep. Years ago a great trouble of sickness had come upon the old red-brick house in Kent; and for long weeks Daisy had been nurse and mother and housewife in one. The evil was defeated at length, but before spreading its wings to fly it revenged itself for her victory over it by striking her down with a long, low fever of weakness.

Energetic Doctor Youth, and quiet, wise old Nurse Nature, hampered a little by the family physician, had soon brought her back to health; but this one characteristic of the illness—this sleep-talking tendency—had lingered with her somewhat obstinately.

The overtired brain, when freed from the controlling influence of the will, seemed not to possess the strength to keep its own counsel.

In the first two or three years after her convalescence, poor Daisy could have had no secret from the little sister who was her bedfellow; and, indeed, had that young lady been so minded, she could have relieved Dick of all anxiety as to his fate at a surprisingly early stage of his courtship.

During the peaceful, untroubled months of her married life, however, the weakness had recurred but rarely, and she was hoping she had conquered it altogether. It is an alarming reflection to the most open of us that, at any moment, we may let it be known what we really think, and Daisy is worried.

"Do I often go on like that?" she asks.

"Not nearly often enough for me," laughs Dick; and then, seeing her evident trouble, "No, no," he adds, "not once in a blue moon, now. You had a headache that night, you know."

"Or perhaps I was suffering from nightmare," suggests Daisy. "I must have been very bad indeed to talk like that."

"Then I shall insist on your always eating hot pork chops for supper," replies Dick. "I like to hear you talk like that."

The gilt clock on the Queen Anne over-mantel strikes nine, and Dick starts, like the well-regulated ghost does at cockcrow,[7] and prepares to depart to a less pleasant place. In Dick's case this undesirable region is the City—that great alchemistic workshop into which middle-class Ambition takes its youth and hope, its heart and brain and life-blood, seeking to melt them into gold.[8]

"You won't be going out at all this evening, Dick?" asks Daisy, as, in the narrow passage, under the little stained-glass gas-lamp, she

---

7   Traditional ghost stories assume that the crowing of the cock is a signal for ghosts to disappear.

8   Dick's association with romantic tales of ghosts and alchemy conflicts with the prosaic nature of his actual job.

stands carefully burnishing the high black helmet, beneath which the nineteenth century knight goes forth to do battle in life's crowded lists.[9]

"No. Why though, any particular reason?"

"Yes. I want you to be here—to help amuse Jessie, you know. By-the-by, Dick, don't you think you'd better bring home one of those donkeys that you pin up against the wall, and then shut your eyes and try to put the tail on; or some game of that sort, that we could play at with her?"[10]

Mrs. Selwyn speaks in a tone of serious consideration; but did her husband see the dancing mischief in her eyes he would understand. Never too prone to quickness of perception, however, and being more intent, at the moment, upon the lighting of a cigarette than upon any other matter, he does not understand.[11]

He argues strongly against his wife's proposal. Jessie must be a biggish girl now, and girls just at that hobbledehoy age are very much offended at being considered children, so he explains; and Daisy gives way, though not without evident disappointment, and the donkey is discarded.

This matter being settled, Dick prepares to take his departure. He and Daisy, more like a pair of guilty lovers than a respectable married couple, both look round to be sure that neither of the two women servants, who with themselves constitute the entire Selwyn establishment,[12] is wandering about within eyeshot. True kisses brook no witnesses. Love, shrinking from the gaze of men, wraps her dark

---

9   The Arthurian legends were widely admired by Jerome's contemporaries.

10   Parlour games such as 'Pin the tail on the donkey' and 'hunt the thimble' were popular with Victorian families and are still played at children's parties today.

11   That Dick smokes in front of his wife denotes their relaxed relationship. Jerome would later remark, 'When the woman smokes her cigarette, while the man pulls at his pipe, they will be better friends. Poetic sentiment may suffer a little, but I think the price is worth it.' (editorial in *To-day*, 19 June 1897)

12   The Selwyns are successful enough to employ two servants, placing them in the respectable but not affluent section of the middle class.

veil around her, and moves through the world unseen. Only in secrecy and silence may she be worshipped.

Rob the religion of Love of its explaining mystery, and it is a meaningless mummery. Drag its sweet observances, its holy rites, into the garish light, and they become mere senseless shows. The spirit of Love is no longer present to consecrate them. They are but as the loud prayers of the Pharisees—mere protestations of respectability.[13]

No one is there to see. Both the domestics, as is evident from their voices, are below, safely out of the way. And so, in the narrow little passage, behind the artistic stained-glass door,[14] Daisy and Dick, as for the first time by the pigstye wall, smile at each other and kiss.

---

13 The Parable of the Pharisee and the Tax Collector. Luke 18:10-14.
'Two men went up to the temple to pray, one a Pharisee and the other a tax collector. The Pharisee stood by himself and prayed: "God, I thank you that I am not like other people—robbers, evildoers, adulterers—or even like this tax collector. I fast twice a week and give a tenth of all I get." But the tax collector stood at a distance. He would not even look up to heaven, but beat his breast and said, "God, have mercy on me, a sinner." 'I tell you that this man, rather than the other, went home justified before God. For all those who exalt themselves will be humbled, and those who humble themselves will be exalted.'

14 Both the 'artistic' door and the thin walls stand as insistent reminders of the Selwyns's respectable status as middle-class dwellers in the suburbs.

34

CHAPTER TWO

Of the Weeds in the Garden

Daisy is a good deal in Dick's thoughts that day. It is Daisy, rather than
the highly-complexioned, foreign-looking maiden who usually adorns
the position, that smiles down upon him from the almanac that hangs
above the office mantelpiece. It is Daisy's value that he sits calculating,
with the market report open before him. He finds himself addressing
the office-boy on one occasion as "dear," under the momentary
illusion that he (the office-boy) is somehow or other Daisy; though
the resemblance would hardly seem sufficient of itself to justify the
mistake.

Dick is junior partner in a small, struggling firm of indigo importers.[1]
Their business is not of colossal proportions just at present; but the
house is young, and youth, though its account in Lombard Street[2] may
remain low, can always keep itself in comfort by drawing on that very
handsome balance which Providence, when she starts her children in
the world, places to each one's credit at the Bank of Hope.

Dick dreams of a day when the British nation will clamour for indigo
faster than it can be supplied to them; so that the firm of Hughliss,
Selwyn & Co., which by then will have risen, guided by its junior
partner's energy and judgement, to the foremost place among the
ranks of indigo importers, will need three special clerks to do nothing
else but enter up its profitable contracts.

---

1   The 'foreign looking maiden' and the indigo importation reference Britain's
successful overseas trade and the imperial enterprise.

2   One of the famous commercial and banking centres in the City of London.

And even when he lays aside the rose-tinted disc, and employs, before the lime-light of imagination that he throws across the future, only the plain glass of common sense, he still sees the prospect very fair before him. Their trade, small though it is, steadily improves; and hard work and perseverance must surely tell more and more in the long run.

He sees the small semi-detached villa which is the present abode of the Selwyn household, give place to a real villa; a villa boldly standing up by itself, needing no support from other villas—a dignified villa, preferring to keep other villas at a certain distance, objecting to familiarity and crowding. A fair-sized garden, which a fond proprietor might, without unreason, allude to as "grounds," encircles the house; and in this garden there are greenhouses, through which a City man on Sunday afternoons might take the City friends who have come down to see his "little place," casually mentioning the while, as a joke against himself, the amount each bunch of grapes or orchid blossom growing there has cost him.

He almost thinks he sees a neat two-horsed brougham waiting before the door. Why should he not? Two-horsed broughams are by no means unknown to the indigo trade.[3]

And, like those of the Irish Princess[4] on her famous walking tour, the robes that Daisy wears are rich and rare; and on her beautiful arms and neck jewels sparkle, like dewdrops upon white lilies. Not that these things will make her seem more fair; only that he will love to give them to her.

Children's voices may enter into the music of their lives.[5] Children's

---

3   Dick is upwardly mobile and unlike Charles Pooter, aspirational.

4   Yseult. The story of the tragic love triangle between King Mark of Cornwall, Tristan and Yseult first appeared in English in about 1300. The story was retold by Victorian poets including Matthew Arnold, Tennyson and Swinburne.

5   Dick's confidence after three years of childless marriage suggests that he and Daisy are probably practising birth control. In 1895 Jerome would claim that 'Prevention, in one form or another, is practised by all the upper classes, and is now as much a recognised custom as marriage itself.' Editorial in *To-day*, 21 December 1895. 210.

children will grow up about them, honouring and loving them. Friends will multiply around them; and the poor shall call them blessed.[6] Thus together, when life's working day is ended, will they pass into the restful twilight of old age.

Not every man can afford to think about the old age of the woman he loves, but to Dick the picture presents no terrors. There are clear-cut, noble faces upon the firm clay of which Time's chisel can only trace faint lines. To such faces, youth and age—like spring and winter to the evergreen—mean but a deeper or a fainter flush. Such a one is Daisy's. Dick sees the fair face grown a little paler, framed in white instead of brown; beside the corners of her mouth he sees a few soft lines, as though the smile that calls so often had sought to save its time by settling down to dwell there; and round her eyes merriment and kindliness, running ever in and out, have left the imprint of their fairy footsteps.

Yes, a very sweet old lady Daisy will be; so Dick thinks. People will say: "What a lovely girl she must have been! How beautiful she is still!"— and "People," usually an addle-headed and untruthful-speaking body, will, for once, say what is right.

Dick takes from one of the drawers of his writing-table a piece of broken looking-glass, and examines his own face therein. He thinks that he himself will not wear badly. Iron-grey hair and a grizzled moustache,[7] he fancies, will rather suit him. Aforesaid people may even say: "What a handsome old couple they make!" Dick is almost impatient for old age.

And, through all changes, they will ever be "Darby and Joan."[8] Dick has no fear that his love for Daisy may fade. He has watched its

6   Possibly an allusion to Psalms 72: 'He shall spare the poor and needy, and shall save the souls of the needy. ... and men shall be blessed in him: all nations shall call him blessed.'

7   The moustache was still fashionable for middle-class men in the 1890s.

8   From a 1735 poem in the *Gentleman's Magazine*: 'Old Darby, with Joan by his side ... They're never happy asunder.'

growth; he knows how deep its roots have struck. He has had time to tell what manner of flower it is. We have fallen into a habit—we men and women—of talking about love as if it were a known quantity—a thing the same, no matter in what heart it may be found. We might as well talk as though we thought Eden capable of producing only one blossom. A man's heart is a garden, upon which God's birds, flying unseen above the world, let fall, one here, one there, the seeds they have picked in the orchards of heaven.

And according to the seed and the ground upon which it lights, so the flower grows. From one heart, a pure white lily rears its stately head; above another, a blood-red poppy bows its sleep-giving cup. Where the ground is poor and uncultivated, there spring forth the daisies and the harebells, the primroses and violets of love, the unpretending, hardy little flowers of the field, whose lowly beauty makes sweet the waste places of the world. And in some soils, where evil things have lain, such growth as comes at all is rank and monstrous.[9]

Very fair the blossoms bloom at first. It is sad to think how many of them quickly droop and die, the ground not being deep enough to give them nourishment.

And of these gardens of ours we ourselves are the gardeners; and whether the seeds planted for us therein thrive or wither depends more on our nurturing or our neglecting than we are prone to think. We are so busy scrambling in the street for happiness, we cannot spare a little time to tend the flowers that make the fragrance of our lives. They will not live uncared for. The earth will close hard and cold about their roots, if we never loosen it a little with the spade of memory. They will shrivel and parch, if we do not wash from their green leaves, now and again, the driving dust of the world. The weeds will grow up and choke them, if we do not watch—the weeds that spring unbidden,

---

9   The narrator comes close to the position of social purity feminists such as Sarah Grand, who believed that moral lapses in the parents would potentially enfeeble the next generation. In effect this made both men and women with a history of sexual deviance unfit to procreate.

whose seeds were let to fall into that human soil many years ago by inexperienced gardener Adam.[10]

Dick's love for Daisy is a plant of sturdy growth. One might liken it, before passing away from the garden simile, to a sprig of heartsease, whose steadfast petals still shine bright when the more brilliant flowers that towered so proudly above it are lying blown and lifeless. The climate of this world is ill-suited to the culture of exotics. Homely plants thrive best down here. It is conceivable that Dante, had he married Beatrice,[11] and, calling his love down from its dwelling-place among the stars, had taken it with him into some Florentine villa, there to expose it to the sordid trivialities, the foolish muddlings and misunderstandings of which our work-a-day life is so full, might have sat wondering to himself one day why he had worshipped her, once upon a time, so devoutly. Romeo, when Juliet's cheek grew furrowed and pale, would no more have longed, one can feel confident, to be the glove upon her hand.[12] If matters had turned out differently, and instead of climbing into her chamber by a rope-ladder, he could have gone upstairs and entered by the door, the probability is very strong that he would have preferred to remain down in the supper-room and make a night of it with Mercutio and other choice spirits of that blend.

Such fevered passions, such ethereal raptures, are the tulips and the lilies of the garden. The sober heartsease long outlives them both.

And Daisy, will her love never fall away from him? What does it cling to—him, or what she *thinks* is him? She could not understand his fear lest some dark, grinning thing, born of himself, might one day stand

---

10   In Genesis Adam and Eve are deceived by the serpent into eating of the fruit of the Tree of Knowledge, and so bring evil into the world.

11   The idealised love of the Italian poet Dante's *Vita Nuova* (ca. 1292-5) and *La Commedia* (completed 1321) became for many commentators a touchstone of the poetic 'ungraspable ideal'.

12   *Romeo and Juliet.* Act 2 scene 2. Again, the narrator suggests that illicit love is both more appealing and more transient than the domestic affection offered by Dick and Daisy's marriage.

beside him, transforming her love to terror. It could not be. She "knew him," — God help them both, he prays, if their lives rest only upon that!

Ah! yes, she " knows" him, as we all "know" each other in this world: as wives know husbands and husbands wives; as lover "knows" lover, and friend "knows" friend; as the shore may "know" the sea. Would she love him if she knew *all* his life? Would her deep, clear eyes look up to his, as they do now, if they could see into his heart—if they could see the evil thoughts that writhe and twine about each other there—the foolish, evil thoughts that, let in youth to run too often in and out, have come, at last, to make the place their home, and will not be forbidden?

Is he, then, worse than other men, he asks himself, or only troubled with a more morbid conscience, that he feels the presence of Daisy's purity at times almost a torture to him, that so often her trusting eyes seem to stab him as with a knife?

He cannot tell. He hopes and believes the latter. Would not the whole world stink if the fair seemings of men were suddenly stripped from them, and their real selves left naked and uncovered to the air? Who can be pure throughout? Yes; women perhaps. Their natures are smaller. There is room in them only for good or evil. But a man's heart is the link between the animalism from which we have sprung and the spiritualism towards which we tend.[13] Let it suffice that we keep our outsides clean; that we watch ever, lest in some weak, fevered moment one of these same small evil thoughts creep out and, reaching the light, become an evil deed, immortal like ourselves.

So he reasons to himself; so he stills to sleep his fear. It is the good that is in him that Daisy loves, and that is hers. The evil that is in him she has never known, and never need know. It has nothing to do with them. It is his alone. Its shadow shall not fall upon their lives.

At five o'clock Dick brushes the dust of the City from his coat,

---

13 The evolution of humanity from the 'animal' to the spiritual and its conflict with atavistic brutal instincts is a persistent theme in Jerome's writing of the 1890s.

washes his hands of all traces of indigo, and sets his face homeward. "Acacia Villa," which is the name that Daisy and he have given to their habitation, in compliment to a dissolute-looking vegetable which occupies the centre of the tiny front garden, and which the local nurseryman has sworn *is* an acacia—a statement which none has ever yet been able either to prove or confute,—is one out of a hundred and fifty-four small red-brick houses, which together make up that quantity known to the postal authorities as "Melina Road, N.W."

They are—to employ the agent's by no means exaggerated description—"charming" little houses. On close inspection, you perceive that each one has made a gallant, though strangely unconvincing, attempt at individuality; while the determination of the whole hundred and fifty-four of them to be, at any rate, "artistic" is evident at the first glance. There is much coloured glass about the doors and windows. There are many white-railed balconies—none of them of the slightest possible use, except perhaps to afford compensation to the cats for the almost entire lack of any roof space practicable for business; and, as regards gables, there is hardly a villa in the road that could not dispute with the homestead described by Nathaniel Hawthorne the sole right to its title.[14]

In each front garden have been planted two small plane trees; and outside in the road, at intervals of ten yards along each sidewalk, grow more plane trees; so that, in summer time, when the sun is shining, Melina Road, N.W., is really, as roads in London suburbs go, a very pleasant road.

But in twilight, or when the rain is falling softly, there is a haunting sadness about its quiet respectability that oppresses the chance passer through with a dull sense of almost physical pain. It feels to him, at such times, as if the whole street were tenanted by silent spectres, living there, behind those artistic curtains, in noiseless gentility.

This evening, as Dick turns into it, the short spring day is drawing

---

14 *The House of the Seven Gables,* a ghost story about the long term effects of evil on subsequent generations (1851).

to a close, and a chill wind makes the bare branches of the trees rattle against each other, with a constant low, tapping sound. He hurries along and reaches his own gate. As he fits the key in the lock, the thought of Jessie recurs to him for the first time since the morning. The recollection irritates him. He will find her sitting in the little front parlour when he enters, and she will rise, silent and very red, to shake hands with him. She will sit between Daisy and himself at dinner, and during the evening, and for four or five evenings to come, he expects, she will have to be talked to and entertained. Again he glances at his mental picture of her--a shy, gawky girl! a little bigger than when he saw her last—a little shyer and gawkier, no doubt.

Thinking thus, he pushes open the door and goes in.

CHAPTER THREE

The Weeds Grow

Nature, in her daily lecture, with demonstrations, upon the wonders of evolution,[1] exhibits to marvelling mankind no more startling change than that resulting from the development of girlhood into womanhood.

A girl at fourteen or fifteen is still in her caterpillar stage. She is, if not a positively disagreeable, at any rate an extremely unattractive object. She is long, and thin, and straight, and colourless. Her movements are slow and clumsy. She is stupid and helpless. Her chief aim in life is to escape attention, and, in this laudable endeavour, her friends and acquaintances do what lies in their power to assist her.

But in a day, the chill spring of youth gives place to the summer of womanhood; and lo! before our dazzled eyes there dances, laughing, a glorious creature of the sun. And our first natural instinct is to follow it, cap in hand, seeking to possess it, so that we may destroy it.

A beautiful, graceful girl rises, smiling, to greet Dick as he enters. It is his turn to be confused and awkward. Can this be Jessie!—this joyous, gold-crowned, soft, white woman,[2] the lank-haired, ungainly, stammering child of three brief years ago!

He takes the hand held out to him, and, holding it, stands staring at her without speaking. Daisy's merry laugh recalls him to himself.

---

1 Educational and scientific lectures were a staple of Victorian entertainment and an alternative to less respectable activities.

2 Pre-Raphaelite painters notably depicted women with pale skin and glorious red hair. The models occupied a marginal position, less than respectable but posed as iconic figures. The narrative insistence on Jessie's pale face and red hair makes her a morally ambiguous Pre-Raphaelite 'stunner'.

"Fine child! isn't it, Dick?"

Dick laughs likewise, but his is a short, nervous laugh.

"I really did not know you," he explains, releasing her hand.

"I thought you didn't," answers Jessie, demurely. "I don't believe he is quite sure about it even now," she adds, turning to Daisy.

"You've changed so," is all that Dick can find to say.

"Wonderful! isn't it, Dick?" remarks Daisy, mockingly. "I suppose nobody ever told you that girls grow up, and become young women?"

"It's you, dear, make me forget that people ever change," he answers, kissing her.

 But not even this pretty speech can buy him off the teasing that Daisy has all day long been saving up for him. Jessie and she, keeping the ball of mischief flying from one to the other, punish him for his stupidity with that delightful plaguing which only girls know how to administer. Daisy, with shameless treachery, reveals to Jessie Dick's reception of the news of her visit—his anxiety as to what they "should do with her," his allusion to her as " a biggish girl" of the "hobbledehoy age." His refusal to bring home, for her amusement, the donkey-and-his-tail game they both agree in attributing to meanness. Jessie says it would have kept her quiet all the evening. As, however, he has objected to afford her this innocent enjoyment, will he, Jessie asks him, play at bears with her, after dinner?[3] That will cost him nothing. Or will he do conjuring tricks?

Jessie is altogether delightful—daringly impudent, saucily sweet. She has just passed into that golden entrance hall, leading from the outer court of girlhood into the temple of womanhood, where the numbing frost of universal snubbing is suddenly exchanged for the expanding warmth of universal homage. For all her life, until a short month or two ago, she has, in common with other tiresome children and awkward girls, been bidden and chidden, lectured and laughed at, taught and

---

3   Representations of idyllic childhood often describe adults pretending to be bears and growling at children. Jessie is innocently unaware of the threat the animalistic Dick poses to her.

tasked, improved, reproved, disproved, but never approved by those near and dear to her; and contemptuously ignored by everybody else. She has awakened one morning to find, as by some magic that she herself as yet can hardly understand, her whole world—or, at all events, the (to her) more interesting portion of it—at her feet. Without her even stretching out her arm to grasp it, the sceptre of authority, that men will fret their lives out to obtain possession of for a few troubled hours, has been placed within her hand. She says to one, "Do this," and he does it, gladly; to another, "Come," and he comes, quickly—the only difficulty being to make him go away again.[4] Her wishes have become rules and regulations, for the guidance of society; her wants, the subject upon which mankind seem most eager for information.

Sayings and doings for which a little while ago she would have been sent to bed, are now considered charming. The wits of the world might well envy the appreciation which her least effort at humour is certain to command. Her novel opinions upon things in general, for the holding of which, had she made them known a year ago, she would have been compelled to write out some silly phrase at least three hundred times, are now welcomed as new and brilliant lights, illumining the dark places of human thought. Elderly, learned men, looking at her through spectacles the while, listen attentively to her views on politics and theology, and become enthusiastically convinced by her arguments upon points that have long appeared doubtful to them; young men, feeling the need of guidance, seek her counsel upon the conduct of life, eager to conform to her ideas, if only she will explain them fully and at as great length as possible. All mankind is in competition to interest and amuse her, to attend her, to serve her, to please her. She is like the little beggar girl in the fairy tale[5] who is, all at once, discovered to be the rightful princess, and who thereupon, exchanging her rags

4   Matthew 8:9, 'For I am a man under authority, having soldiers under me: and I say to this man, Go, and he goeth; and to another, Come, and he cometh; and to my servant, Do this, and he doeth it.'

5   Loretta Ellen Brady. 'The Beggar Princess' in *The Green Forest Fairy Book* (1892).

3: THE WEEDS GROW

for a costly dress, embroidered with diamonds and rubies, ascends the throne amid the joyful acclamations of the people.

And the little beggar girl, no longer harried and neglected, but honoured and adored, soon lets fall her shyness and her awkwardness, to take up in their place gaiety and confidence; so that those who knew her in her earlier days say: "Dear me! How Goody No Shoes *has* altered, to be sure!"[6]

Dick having been sufficiently tormented, is allowed quarter, and the talk travels to the old red-brick Kentish house and its neighbourhood.

"How is Captain Cuttle,[7] the old three-legged Tomcat?" asks Daisy; "and does he fight now as much as ever, or has age sobered the hot, fierce passions of his youth? Is the curate still single, or has he at last capitulated, and if so, to which of the seventeen? How did the yeomanry ball go off? and who is Bertha engaged to, now?"

Jessie gives to Daisy's many questions, jesting rejoinders; and then goes on to tell the further news and gossip of the mid-Kent world. A very amusing world it seems, judging from her talk of it. Over its squabbles and mishaps, its vexations and imbroglios, she makes very merry. All life to her just now is one great comedy, being played so that she may laugh.

"And how do you like being grown-up?" asks Dick, upon the conclusion of her naive account of how, in consequence of her having remarked at a party on the thirteenth of February that she loved fox-terriers, four of those unruly quadrupeds had been left anonymously at the house during the course of the next day, to the intense disgust of her aunt, who neither knew what to do with them nor where to send them back.

"Oh, it's just delightful!" replies Jessie, with a meaning nod of her head.

"Anybody been making love to you?" he continues, with the

---

6   An allusion to *The History of Little Goody Two-Shoes* (1765).

7   A benevolent former sea captain in Dickens's *Dombey and Son* (1846-48).

indifference of the married man towards the sentimentalities that agitate the heart of youth.

"Oh, Dick!" exclaims Daisy, reprovingly, "don't put such ideas into the child's head."

Daisy is Jessie's senior by four years, and, therefore, naturally assumes a somewhat motherly attitude towards her.

"Have they?" persists Dick, mischievously.

Jessie blushes slightly and laughs.

"Oh, they are very silly, some of them!" she explains, vaguely.

"Very silly!" repeats Dick, in tones of pretended indignation. "And that is how a modern girl describes her adorers!"[8]

"It's a very correct description of them, I expect," remarks Daisy, sententiously.

"Is Barnard very silly?" asks Dick.

Barnard, it should be mentioned, is a cousin of Jessie's who used, so the family gossips asserted, "to be a little sweet" upon her. They were brought up together as children, a circumstance which, in the days of her unpromising girlhood, was held to explain his otherwise unaccountable affection for her. Dick knows nothing of the young fellow's present attitude towards her, but he assumes, not unreasonably, that anyone who admired Jessie three years ago would be her admirer still.

"Oh, Barnard!" replies Jessie, unconsciously assuming with the subject a tone of proprietorship. "Oh, he doesn't count! He's just like a brother."

"Ah, you've never had any real brothers, my dear," laughs Daisy, "or you wouldn't think so."

Daisy has three of her own, and considers the comparison ill-founded.

---

8   Jokes about the modern woman's supposed contempt for men and marriage were topical at this time. Mona Caird's controversial article on 'Marriage' published in the *Westminster Review* in August 1888 had led to a long running debate in the *Telegraph* on the subject 'Is marriage a failure?' See also Appendix D on p. 97.

"They are very nice, those sort of brothers, aren't they, Jessie?" continues Dick. "Have you got any more of them?"

"Not yet," she replies, with audacious frankness, "but I could do with a few. Do you know any quiet, well-behaved young men who want to be adopted?"

Dick laughs, and Daisy sighs.

"Oh dear! they have been bringing you up badly, Jessie, since I left," she says. "Dick, don't encourage her. It's really quite shocking."

"We are both very much ashamed of you," Dick takes it upon himself to explain, with reproving gravity.

Jessie replies by a look of mock contrition; and then proceeds to enquire after Dick's general behaviour.

Daisy, for answer, draws out a merry indictment against him, and appeals to Jessie for sympathy; whereupon Dick, in retaliation, enumerates, amid a running commentary of such ejaculations as "Oh, Dick! how can you?" "Oh, I don't! You do exaggerate!" "Don't believe him, Jessie!" Daisy's manifold misdeeds, and also appeals to Jessie for sympathy.

But the thought that, as he lightly laughs and jests, lies all the time, at the bottom of his mind, like mud at the bottom of a rippling stream, is: How wonderfully white! how wonderfully soft she is!

At dinner he has more opportunity of watching her unobserved. He notes the well-poised, dainty head; the full, firm throat; the rounded wrist, looking, as it escapes beyond the close fitting sleeve, like fruit from which the peel has been pushed back.

Once, as he renders her some small service of the table, his hand, by chance, touches hers, and he feels the hot blood mount swiftly to his face. He bends his head down low, and stealthily glances across, fearing lest Daisy may have noticed the flush—a needless fear, as he tells himself the next moment: even had she seen, she would not have understood.

During the evening, Daisy asks Jessie to sing, and Jessie readily enough consents. She knows that she possesses a beautiful voice, and she is nothing loath to display her accomplishments before Dick. Indeed, she is particularly anxious to impress him, above all other men, with a sense of her present attractions. Dick knew her when she was a despised, uninteresting personage, and had, she shrewdly suspects, no particular liking for her; and, before those who were acquainted with our poverty, it is particularly gratifying to display our wealth.

"Open the piano, and light the candles, and get me my music," she saucily commands Dick, and in the same breath she adds to Daisy: "You don't mind my ordering him about, do you, dear? You shall come and order my husband about when I'm married."

"Poor fellow!" laughs Daisy. "He will have enough on his hands if he has to attend to any more orders than yours."

Dick obeys, and then, taking his stand beside her, essays to turn the music for her. Jessie's songs, however, are elaborate compositions, demanding much precision and rapidity in their execution, and Dick's limited knowledge renders his efforts at assistance more of a hindrance than a help. Daisy, perceiving the trouble, comes to the rescue, and, taking her place at the other side of the piano, relieves him of his task. But notwithstanding this, he still maintains his position, which commands new views of Jessie.

As they are grouped thus, Daisy stretches out her disengaged hand behind Jessie, shyly seeking Dick's. He clasps it in his and holds it, wondering if, supposing things were the other way round, and it were Jessie and he who were one, and Daisy the stranger, crossing their life, he should be now standing, fondling Jessie's hand, and trying, by the aid of his imagination, to make it do duty for Daisy's.

Jessie, on rising from the piano, insists on Daisy's contributing her share to the concert. Daisy's musical *répertoire* is one that superior persons, of whom there seem to be a considerable number about just at present, would deem trite and vulgar, but to Dick's uncultured ear the quaint old ballads and love-songs are still heart-satisfying. He seats himself comfortably in an easy-chair opposite Jessie, and gives himself up to the deep contentment that steals over him as he listens. Daisy's voice is a wind that never fails to stir the tendrils of his heart. Its soft caressing notes vibrate through his being, waking echoes of love and tenderness. How sweet! how fair! she is, he thinks. How good it is of God to have given to him this gentle spirit to shed brightness on his life! In this moment, his nature asks only one other thing to complete its perfect happiness—and that is, that he should be pressing his lips against the white shapely hand that is resting idly on the rail of the chair opposite to him.

Jessie pleads tiredness early in the evening, and, wishing Dick good-night, retires. Daisy accompanies her upstairs, to be sure that the spare room has been made comfortable for her, and Dick is left alone.

As the door closes behind the two girls, the frank, boyish-looking Dick disappears, as a mask that is taken off and laid aside; and a bent man, with an old, evil face, sits looking down into the fire.[9]

The door opens quietly, and Jessie enters the room.

"Hulloa," says the man by the fire, starting up, but not looking round at her; "come down again?"

"Yes; I've forgotten my watch-key. Will yours fit?"

"We'll try. Where's Daisy?"

"Upstairs. —— Thanks. Good-night."

"Good-night."

He takes her hand, and holds it for an instant. How soft, how cool it feels! and his lips are so dry and parched.

He glances up at her, and their eyes meet. Has something told her his thought? Is it only the reflection from the coloured glass of the little gas-lamp, swaying to and fro in the passage without, that passes across her face? Is it only his fancy that her hand is trembling?

"Good-night," he says again, as she quietly withdraws it. "Hope you'll sleep well."

---

9   Readers would have picked up on the echo of R. L. Stevenson's gothic novella *Jekyll and Hyde*, published in 1886. In Stevenson's text the protagonist is tortured by the co-existence of two sides of his personality and misguidedly tries to separate them.

"I think I shall. Good-night."

Daisy comes back after a little while shivering, and stoops down before the fire to warm herself.

"Isn't she pretty?" she asks, spreading her hands before the dying embers.

"Yes," replies Dick, dreamily.

Daisy stands up, and draws his arm around her.

"Poor old boy," she says. "You're looking worried. Anything happened to trouble you, dear?"

Dick turns and looks down at her.

"No," he answers; "I was thinking, that was all."

Then he puts both his arms around her, and presses her to him tighter and tighter; as if he would hold her so close that nothing could ever come between them—not even so slim a thing as the shadow of an evil thought.

CHAPTER FOUR

The Vigilance of the Husbandman

Jessie remains a guest at Acacia Villa for about a week; and day by day the evil looks out bolder and bolder at her from Dick's eyes, and beneath its hot glance there springs to life within her, as unclean things are born of tropic waters by the noonday sun, a tiny growth of answering desire.

A very weakly growth it is, as yet—a weed that might, by anyone that knew it was a weed, be plucked up by the roots with ease and cast aside; that might by some poor child, ignorant of its genus, lustful of all life, never doubting that all gifts the gods may send are good, be left to spread its baneful leaves above the soil, poisoning the garden for all future flowers.

Thus an understanding, unspoken of by either, unacknowledged to themselves, comes to exist between them. Thus in the brightly-lighted little drawing-room, in the bustling street, in the crowded theatre, in all places and at all times there comes to be a secret chamber of dark thought, whose door swings softly open at the meeting of their eyes, and into which, one beckoning, the other following fearfully, they steal, and close the door noiselessly behind them, leaving Daisy talking and laughing to the empty air without.

And nothing is done, and nothing is said, and nothing is meant, that even that dragon of virtue, Mrs. Grundy[1] herself, could see any impropriety in. For Evil is a spirit, and can and does—with no

---

1   A character in Thomas Morton's 1798 play *Speed the Plough* and a byword for prudery in Victorian culture. Jokes about Mrs Grundy were comparable to the twentieth-century 'What will the neighbours say?'

doubt many an inward chuckle—make itself invisible to human eyes, especially to the eyes of great and good Mrs. Grundy, who, peace-loving old lady, only asks of it that it *shall* make itself invisible.

For after all, as Dick argues to himself, with a comforting shrug of the shoulders, what is there in it? A little longer pressure than need be perhaps of palm to palm, a mere kiss of the hand, or, maybe, of the rounded wrist above the hand! Dick has kissed another woman's hand at other times, and Daisy has stood by laughing. Only now, when he kisses Jessie's hand, he makes sure first that Daisy is *not* standing by.

The draught in the cup is harmless enough: it is their lips that poison it. The spirit of evil lurks ever behind them, tainting with its breath all things that come to them, charging each little act of courtesy, each trivial privilege of friendship, with secrecy and meaning.

Dick will be standing in the drawing-room, buttoning Jessie's glove. Surely an innocent civility this! One that Sir Galahad[2] himself might have tendered had damsels worn eight-buttoned gloves in the days of his pilgrimage. Yet at the sound of Daisy's step outside, they both start, and move swiftly away from one another; and when Daisy opens the door, Dick is stooping down poking the fire, so that he does not turn his face towards her for a little while, and Jessie is watching very intensely something out in the street, and does not come away from the window until the something has passed out of sight.

One evening, at supper, Jessie's hand rests on the table near to Dick's, and, Daisy having risen to get some small thing from the sideboard, he puts his over it and holds it, talking the while to Daisy. She turns round somewhat quickly. There is no time to draw his hand away, but, cat-like, in an instant he changes its attitude, trying to make its position seem mere chance; and then, with white, dry face not daring to look up, sits waiting for the sound of Daisy's voice.

Her first few words tell him that she has noticed nothing, but he and Jessie do not look at each other again all that evening; and Dick that

2   One of the knights of the Round Table, Sir Galahad was the son of Sir Lancelot and renowned for his purity.

night, while Daisy sleeps, lies listening to a very serious lecture from that very wise old lady, Mrs. Worldly Prudence.

It is not a very ennobling voice, the voice of Worldly Prudence; but it is, perhaps, none the less practically influential on that account. It is, generally speaking, on the side of virtue; and it saves the world from more sin in a week than the still small voice of Conscience—so unnecessarily still, so painfully weak—does in a century.

Against people that mount pulpits and preach at us, we instinctively shut our ears. Worldly Prudence draws her chair up opposite ours, and, trying to look severe, shakes her head at us; and we laugh back deprecatingly, and prepare to listen to her. About the right or wrong of it she troubles neither her head nor our heart. What she says, kindly, is: "My dear boy"—or girl, as the case may be—"is this wise? Is the game worth the candle?"[3]

And in the majority of cases the dear old lady is able to show us very clearly that it is not; and so we go and sin no more.

Says Worldly Prudence to Dick:

"Dick, don't you be a fool. Don't you risk your whole life's happiness for the gratification of a few chance moments. Look at this thing practically, lad. You love your wife very dearly, and she loves you. Is it worth while to imperil a bliss such as most men only dream of, to court a misery such as you dare not think upon, for—what? The passing touch of a girl's hand, the pressure of your lips for an instant against a bit of soft white flesh! You know what Daisy is—as good and sweet a little woman as ever breathed. But, my dear Dick, she has not our—what shall I say? our broad views. She does not understand the world like you and I do. She would not regard your—what shall we call it?—your flirtation with the same leniency that might be extended towards it by a more experienced, or, so far as these matters go, a more sympathetic wife. Don't be a fool, Dick. Let that little incident of to-night serve as a warning to you. End this nonsense before mischief

---

3   A phrase first used in English in the late seventeenth century. Literally the game is not worth the expense of lighting a candle.

comes of it."

And Dick, like a drunken man suddenly sobered by some near
escape from danger, determines to give way no more to the evil that
has so nearly been his ruin; and thereupon, feeling himself already a
reformed character, falls asleep.

Jessie, never having had the advantage of an introduction to Dame
Worldly Prudence, receives, however, no visit from that excellent
counsellor of mankind; and, knowing nothing of her confab[4] with
Dick, finds his greatly altered manner somewhat puzzling. She does
not approve of the change. Those sly admiring glances, those little
covert tendernesses from an extremely agreeable and good-looking
young man were by no means unacceptable. That the receipt of them
was attended by a certain amount of danger; that the things given
were, in strictness, the property of somebody else, only added to them
a pleasant piquancy. A very weak voice has, it is true, whispered to
her now and again that such glances, such tendernesses, would hardly
be proffered by a perfectly honourable married man to his wife's
cousin,—would hardly be permitted by a perfectly honourable cousin
from a cousin's husband. But, as she has answered (and thereupon
gone away quickly without waiting for further reply), Dick is nothing
more to her than a big brother. He means nothing more than to shew
her brotherly affection. She means nothing more than to repay him
with sisterly kindness.

Besides, life is so full, and the world is so sweet; there really is not
time to do anything more than hold one's hands out to the gods and
laugh.

Dick, seeing the waiting look in Jessie's eyes, finds the temptation
somewhat harder to combat than he had anticipated, it being supported
by an ally he had not reckoned for. Worldly Prudence, however, loyally
keeps by his side, and with her aid he holds his ground, until the last
day of Jessie's visit arrives, bringing with it, to him, much sense of
relief.

---

4   Slang for confabulation, i.e. conversation.

She is going down to Kent by an evening train, and Daisy suggests that Dick should go with her in the cab to Charing Cross and see her off.

"Come with us, then, Daisy," says Dick; "we shall have to take a four-wheeler for the box.[5] Let us both go."

Daisy, however, has some needlework to do, and does not think she ought to spare the time.

So a four-wheeled cab is sent for, and Jessie's trunk is put up on the roof; and Jessie and Dick get into it alone, Daisy waving good-bye to them from the steps.

"Never mind the needlework," cries Dick to her, putting his head out of the window. "Slip on your jacket, and come!"

But Daisy, laughing, shakes her head, and the cab scrunches away into the darkness.

Daisy wishes the next moment that she had gone. Somehow, the empty house behind her seems dreary and ghostlike. But it is too late to stop them now. She steps back into the passage and closes the door.

It is a long drive from Melina Road, N.W., to Charing Cross. For some distance neither Jessie nor Dick speak to one another. At last Dick says:

"It will be sometime, then, before we next see you?"

"Yes; I don't suppose I shall come up to London again before I go abroad."

"How long do you expect to be abroad?"

"Oh! about a year—unless they come to the conclusion that my voice isn't worth it."

"Don't go and marry a German."

Jessie laughs.

"Do you think one of them is likely to ask me?"

"Yes."

Dick's tone is somewhat more serious than the nature of the conversation would seem to demand.

---

5   Jessie's luggage is a precursor of the modern suitcase.

Jessie does not reply for a little while. Then, looking out of the window, she says shortly, in a low voice:

"Why?"

"Because you'll be the most beautiful woman that he has ever seen."

Dick's voice sounds strangely far off to Jessie, though she feels the breath of it upon her neck. She sits leaning forward, still looking out upon the wet night. He puts his arm around her, and draws her to him, taking her gloved hand in his.

Worldly Prudence is not beside him during this ride. Really, as the good lady has told herself, there was no need for her to accompany him. The night is very dark, and the interior of a four-wheeled cab is very dark; and Daisy waits by the fireside at Acacia Villa. Worldly Prudence feels that under these circumstances she need not trouble herself concerning her *protégé*.

Poor little easily-snubbed Conscience ventures to gently reprove him once or twice; but he explains to her that this is the last occasion on which he will see Jessie for a very long period. Many things will have happened before they meet again. They will have had time to grow indifferent to each other. This passing passion of his must end with the day: to-morrow the object of it will be far away. No hurt can come from indulging it just a little to-night—to a harmless, circumspect degree, that is.

Let him enjoy the cakes and ale for this last time, and henceforth he will be virtuous and never taste them more. And Conscience, doubtful from experience, but desirous above all things not to seem disobliging, pretends to be contented with the bargain.

The cab reaches Oxford Street, and, crossing it, plunges noisily into dingy Soho. As they turn a corner, the flaring light from a public house flashes through the window, shewing them each for an instant the other's face;[6] then darts out, leaving the kindly darkness to wrap them

---

6   In *Novel Notes* (1892) the narrator describes a dream in which 'I saw a woman's face among a throng. It is an evil face, but there is a strange beauty in it. The flickering gleams thrown by street lamps flash down upon it, showing the wonder of its evil

round again. Dick draws her, trembling, to him, and in the darkness their lips meet.

But only for an instant. Conscience standing by, fearful, plucks Dick by the sleeve, and the kiss is left unfinished. Better perhaps for both if it had been completed—if they had drained the cup then and there to the dregs and tasted the lees. The first sip leaves so sweet a flavour in the mouth: one is apt not to rest satisfied with it.

He lets her hand go, and they sit apart, each wondering what the other is thinking. The cab jolts and rattles on through the wet, glistening streets. The yellow rays from the gas-lamps and the shops as they pass by steal in and look at them, and glide away.

They reach Charing Cross some twenty minutes before Jessie's train goes, and the time seems rather long to Dick. They walk up and down the platform, and he tries to talk to her; but she bores him. She is clever and witty; she is ever full of life and good spirits. Her talk is always fresh and piquant, her laugh is ready and musical, her chaff is saucy and bewitching. But she bores him; mere open, friendly converse with her generally does bore him. Her girlish fascinations, her womanly charms of mind and manner, are no more to him than are the song and plumage of the bird to the hawk: who is, nevertheless, very fond of little birds.

Many men would have given much for that twenty minutes' promenade with her that so bores Dick. Many people might have found it interesting to talk to little Red Riding Hood,[7] and to listen to her childish prattle. To the wolf the conversation must have been a very tiresome effort.

Besides, he is thinking of Daisy, and is longing to get back to her. It seems an age since they had one of their pleasant evening chats together, planning out delightful futures, building fair castles in the air. He sees her waiting for him by the fireside at home. He sees her sweet,

---

fairness. ' 42-44. See Appendix B on p. 86.

7   Modern critics have highlighted the possible interpretation of the Little Red Riding Hood story as a warning against seduction.

pure face light up with its ever-new smile of welcome as he enters. Will this twenty minutes never go!

It comes to an end at last. They shake hands through the carriage window, and say "Good-bye." He remains standing on the platform until the curve in the line makes it impossible for Jessie, should she be looking out, to tell if he is still there or not. Then he hurries away.

He takes a cab home. It is a piece of extravagance he would not under ordinary circumstances permit himself; but to-night he feels that small change is not to be reckoned against the minutes saved in getting back to Daisy's side.

She rises to meet him as he opens the door of the little parlour, and comes forward with just the smile that he has pictured to himself. He takes her hands and kisses her. Somehow, it seems to him that he has been away a long, long time.

He sits down over against her by the fire and watches her. How sweet, how noble, life appears in the light of her pure presence. How poor and jangling evil voices sound amid the music of her love.

"It seems quite strange, the house now, without Jessie," she says, taking up the work she had laid down. "Isn't she delightful?"

"Yes," he replies; "but it's pleasant to be quite by ourselves again, isn't it?"

She answers by one of those beautiful tender looks that Heaven sends sometimes into a woman's eyes to prepare us for the sight one day of Love itself.

He goes over and, sinking down beside her, hides his face in her lap—just as, years ago, in the days of childish sorrows and childish sins, he used to lay his little troubled head upon his mother's knee.

CHAPTER FIVE

The Negligence of the Husbandman

Thus Jessie, with her white arms and red-gold hair, passes away out of Dick's life, leaving only the memory of her to trouble his peace of mind.

Unfortunately, the memory is somewhat vivid and seems inclined to linger, so that poor Dick's heart, or rather that department of it where dwell such emotions as are born of white arms and red-gold hair, still continues, in consequence, a little agitated—like heaving waters haunted by the memory of a wind.

Perhaps he does not wish to quite forget her. It is rather pleasant to be able to take her with him now and again into the shady paths of thought. The straight, level road of strict propriety is apt to become after a while uninteresting to the average male pedestrian. Estimable travellers upon its even surface are occasionally seized by wild yearnings to break through its well-kept hedges, and take a brief, mad holiday in the tempting fields beyond. To the estimable traveller who does not care to pay the penalty exacted by a moral world as the price for such excursions, a lively imagination is of much service. He himself is the hero and Jessie the heroine of many romances that Dick dreams out to himself—romances not for publication.

His conscience takes exception to these works of fiction, and he finds it necessary to excuse himself. Conscience talks to him of gentlemen who are loyal even in thought to the women they love. Dick answers that these exemplary lovers and husbands are mostly met with in novels—written by ladies. Conscience, growing more serious, quotes the Scriptures. Dick thinks it well that human laws are less rigid: thinks the Courts might be inconveniently crowded were it otherwise.

At other times, and when in other moods, Dick, siding with his conscience, takes himself severely to task, and works himself up into a most laudable state of moral indignation against himself. As a result of which, he determines to put all unruly thoughts away from him.

But unruly thoughts, the spoilt children of our brain, are very difficult to rule. We allowed them to have their own way too much when young. No kind, motherly friend advised us or warned us. We let them grow up uncurbed. They are somewhat apt to rule us now.

Dick trusts that Time will help him: Jessie's image will grow fainter to his vision in spite of himself. Under any circumstances, it is comforting to reflect that no practical harm can result. Jessie is far away, in a few weeks' time will be still farther. Evil thought is a dangerous pet. It is safer to play with it from behind the iron bars of circumstance.

Letters from Jessie arrive at Acacia Villa pretty frequently now—letters to Daisy,—in which Jessie talks chiefly about herself, and Daisy reads extracts from them to Dick across the breakfast-table. From hints that Jessie lets fall, it would appear that Barnard's attentions and intentions are growing unmistakably pronounced. The old married couple at Acacia Villa discuss the situation. Both agree that Barnard would make an excellent husband for Jessie. Especially has he recommended himself to Daisy by his faithfulness—faithfulness in a lover being a virtue highly esteemed by every woman, except the woman beloved. Both hope Jessie's regard for him will ripen into love—as, indeed, why should it not? probability being certainly in favour of such a result.

One day Dick is returning home a little later than usual. A chill autumn wind meets him as he turns the corner of Melina Road, while the all-important "It," by whose two letters we designate the world's complicated atmospheric machinery commences that unpleasant operation popularly referred to as "trying to rain"—as though it were to be supposed that the English weather were inexperienced in the matter of raining, and at times wanted to rain, but did not know how to do it.

The evening reminds him of the evening of Jessie's first visit to Acacia Villa, and sets him thinking of her. He is thinking of her as he hangs up his hat and coat in the little hall. As he opens the parlour door, he struggles to put the thought of her away, and succeeds in doing so just in time to take Daisy in his arms and kiss her.

Daisy has an open letter in her hand.

"What do you think?" she says. "Jessie is coming to spend a fortnight with us before she goes abroad. I wrote and asked her to try and manage it, but I was afraid she would not be able to. I am so glad!"

The fading daylight in the room is very dim, or Daisy would see opposite to her a white face, staring before it with a frightened look, as if it saw grinning at it from out of the gloom some fearful thing that it could not escape from.

"Can't you put her off?" he says, still with his eyes fixed upon the thing he sees. "Tell her I have to be away. Let us go away together for a little while. I want a holiday. Let us go away together, Daisy—together." He turns to her and takes her in his arms. "You and I together, Daisy, and nothing—nothing—to come between us. You and I, wife; you and I!"

He presses her to him with a grasp that almost hurts her. She looks at him bewildered and alarmed.

"What is the matter, Dick?" she cries. "Dear one, there is something wrong! What is it? Tell me!"

Ah! if he only could. If, holding her there close to him in the darkness, he could only say: "Daisy, Daisy, little white-souled wife of mine, you do not know me. You have never known me. Know me now, and help me! Oh, Daisy! my heart is full of evil—evil thoughts and evil passions. I have let them grow unchecked, and now they are deep-rooted, and I cannot pluck them out. Help my weakness with the strength of your purity. Help my choked prayer with your clear voice. And Daisy dear; Daisy, little sweetheart, that God knows I love, keep this girl, with her soft flesh and her rounded form, away from my eyes!"

But the cry reaches his lips only to die away in silence. She would not understand. How could she understand? Can the dove understand the tiger? Between King David[1] and the angels there could have been no sympathy. They would never have said of him that he was a man after their own heart. They could never have understood or pitied him.

She would start away from him in terror and loathing. "You are *that*, and I have loved you! You are that thing, and our lips have met! You say you love me. 'Tis a lie; you have never loved me! *Your* love! It has been an outrage, a foul insult, put upon me! God forgive you, never let me see your face again!"

Safe within the walled city of her innocence, she knows nothing of that fierce, silent battle-field where, day and night, the forces of good and evil sway to and fro, contending with each other.

The Garden of Eden is still open to mankind. Hidden away from the dust of the world, its pleasant places still are green, its limpid streams still flow. Still, each man and woman God creates He places there, saying: "Of every tree of the garden thou mayst freely eat. But of the tree of knowledge of good and evil, thou shalt not eat of it."[2] For in the day that we eat of that tree we are driven out of the garden, and in sorrow wander all the days of our lives, and its peaceful glades we never tread again.

Daisy has passed the fatal tree untempted. She has never plucked the wisdom-giving fruit. She knows not evil. To her it is a foul thing, outlawed from God's world—a thing apart, abiding in strange places of its own. That it could have its dwelling around her in the hearts of those she loved; that it could live there side by side with good, the one sleeping while the other watched, she would deem monstrous and impossible. Seeing the good, she thinks no evil. Shew her the evil, and the good would seem to her only a mocking mask.

---

1   In the Old Testament King David is described as committing adultery with Bathsheba, wife of Uriah the Hittite. Samuel 11:1016

2   Genesis 2:16-17 And the LORD God commanded the man, saying, Of every tree of the garden thou mayest freely eat: But of the tree of the knowledge of good and evil, thou shalt not eat of it: for in the day that thou eatest thereof thou shalt surely die.

"No, dear; there's nothing wrong," he answers, turning away. "Don't take any notice of me. I feel worried and irritable, that's all; and as if I didn't want the task of entertaining visitors. My liver's out of order, I expect."

He laughs, and, crossing to the fireplace, stirs the sinking embers with his foot. Daisy follows, and puts her arm round his neck.

"Poor old thing," she croons, drawing his face down to hers and kissing him. "It will feel better in a day or two. And Jessie isn't a visitor, you old stupid. Come and have your dinner. It's quite late."

So again there comes an evening when Dick, opening the drawing-room door, sees this same soft, white woman, holding out her hand to him.

But the saucy frankness of her former greeting has vanished. In its place there wraps itself around her an air of shrinking and constraint. Her hand, as his touches it, trembles, and he lets it fall hurriedly and somewhat awkwardly. They exchange a few commonplace questions and remarks without looking at one another; and then, feeling themselves sliding down into an abyss of silence, both turn and cling, conversationally, to Daisy for support.

After dinner, Dick suggests a visit to one of the exhibitions, and Daisy, explaining that she has not been feeling very well for the last few days, asks them to go without her.

"Oh no," replies Dick; "I shouldn't care to go without you. We'll leave it for tonight."

"Oh, but I wish you would," argues Daisy. "It's a shame for me to keep you in. And I shall be so glad to get rid of you both."

But Dick remains obdurate; and Daisy continuing to urge him, he grows vehement and almost angry. There are hours enough before him when he will stand beside this woman's beauty, with a tempting devil whispering in his ear and no help near but his own feeble strength. Daisy's voice can raise up around him a sanctuary into which Lucifer and his angels may not follow. He will not venture forth before need be.

The protection of her presence fails him, however, as the days go
by even more than he had feared. The weakness of which she has for
some time past been complaining (if such a term as "complaining" can
be applied to laughing apologies for a trifling deficiency in the usually
overflowing measure of helpfulness and gaiety dealt out to those
around her) has been declared by the leading doctor of the Melina
Road neighbourhood to be the result of a slight nervous disorder—the
aftermath perhaps of her long illness of four years ago—demanding
for its cure rest and quiet; and Dick and Jessie are, in consequence,
thrown much alone together.

What is poor, frail man to do when the Fates combine against him,
but let himself drift down the current into which they have laughingly
tossed him, trusting that they will not, in their good-nature, altogether
drown him; but that, when they have had their sport with him, they
will allow him to struggle to the shore and scramble out, panting but
thankful.

After all, is he not troubling himself too much about this thing, Dick
asks himself. Is he not making the danger greater by his fear of it?
Are not his very struggles entangling him tighter in the net? May not
passions, like noxious gases, be less productive of ill if permitted an
occasional circumscribed escape into the air, if not too sternly driven
underground? May not a tempting voice, like a woman's tongue, weary
itself the sooner the more it be left to talk uncontradicted, undisputed
with?

Besides, a man may surely flirt a little with his wife's pretty cousin;
may surely even bestow upon her a little mild affection without feeling
that he is outraging the laws of God and man. He has been setting
himself too high a standard in this matter; that has been the trouble.
He has been taking too severe a view of his own shortcomings.

What has he ever done? What is there any fear that he would ever do,
but "carry on"[3] a little with a jolly girl? Dick gains much satisfaction

---

3   Jerome was often denigrated in the press for his use of slang terms. The use of
quotation marks here is a reminder that while he often used colloquial speech in his

by dressing his thoughts in a colloquial garb. Words are coloured spectacles through which we look at facts. All things take their tint from the terms in which we speak of them. "Carry on" conveys a suggestion of innocent, if slightly vulgar, playfulness. It is quite impossible that there can be any actual harm in "carrying on."

Put any other young fellow in his place, and that other young fellow would undoubtedly, so Dick assures himself after reflection, behave in precisely the same manner that has seemed to his own troublesome conscience exceedingly reprehensible. Indeed, so evident does this appear to him that he almost feels that he has been acting somewhat snobbishly in seeking to be superior to all these other fellows.

Ah! these "other people"—these "other men"—these "other women"—why will they persist in setting us bad examples? We do so many things we should not do, just because they do them. We leave undone so many things we should do, just because they do not do them.[4] Really, it would be only fair if, now and then, they had to share with us the penalty.

Dick experiences much more ease of mind after this discussion with himself. He feels that he has swept aside the web of morbid fancies that was obscuring the subject, and has let in upon it the light of common sense.

Only one disquieting reflection remains to him, and that is that were Daisy ever to see this thing—ever, in some moment of mischance, to catch a glimpse of it where it silently crouches within the shadowy places of their life, which God forbid!—*she* would not see it in the light of common sense.

Dick and Jessie go about a good deal together, to places of amusement, to picture-galleries and exhibitions, for walks and shopping excursions, she having to purchase many things in London before leaving. Daisy

---

fiction, he did so in order to characterise particular speakers.

4   The prayer of confession used at the beginning of the Church service: 'We have left undone those things which we ought to have done; And we have done those things which we ought not to have done.'

remains at home, and laughingly greets them when they return, and chats with them about where they have been and what they have seen. She hopes Jessie does not think it unkind of her, not being able to accompany them; and Jessie, carefully avoiding Dick's eyes, answers: "Oh no, dear, of course not. I'm only so sorry you are not well enough."

To Dick, when she is alone with him, she apologises for not being able to take her share in the duty of entertaining and chaperoning Jessie. She fears it must be rather a nuisance to him having his time so much taken up. She is a bad girl, isn't she, to go and get ill during this particular fortnight? she asks him, laying her head a little tiredly against his shoulder. Dick pats her cheek and kisses her, wincing a little.

The relationship between himself and Jessie has, after a few days' feeble fencing with inclination on both sides, been resumed at the point at which it was broken off six months ago, and though the position has not been advanced, it has been strengthened. Words and caresses that were then doubtfully ventured upon and timorously received, now pass as current coin between them. His hand seeks hers, hers gives itself to his, as a natural thing, whenever opportunity allows. She renders to him a trembling yielding in all things. He does not ask himself the cause. Perhaps he fears too much the explanation.

She is to him a wondrous untried instrument, whose delicious music waits only the musician's hand. It is sweet to play upon it, to draw forth the hidden harmonies that rise responsive to his touch. It is sweet to whisper daring questions in her ear, and to catch the fainting answer from her lips; sweet to look down the depths of her dark eyes, and watch her shamed heart trying to hide itself from his sight.

Yet he is careful not to go "too far," as he would term it. He measures himself out this thing, as a respectability-loving toper,[5] conscious of his own weakness, permits himself just so much and no more of his favourite spirit as he knows he can safely take. Recognising that he has to think for both, he is even more circumspect than he might otherwise deem necessary. Compared with what might be, he feels himself, under

---

5   Tippler.

all the circumstances, to be quite a modern Joseph.[6]

There are times, it is true, when—in thought, at all events—he falls away somewhat from this high standard. There are moments when, gazing at her radiant youth and beauty, all things in earth and heaven seem light when weighed in the balance against one long, clinging kiss upon her red lips.

But he promptly beats down these unlicensable emotions. He will be true to the ideal he has set himself. He will permit himself nothing but what his instinct tells him the average man would likewise allow himself.

One evening something prompts him to take a less narrow view than usual of the average man's privileges. They have returned home late from the theatre to find that the rest of the small household have retired for the night. Daisy had dismissed the servants, meaning to sit up for them by herself; but, her weakness growing upon her, she has been compelled to follow them to bed, leaving a pencilled note upon the supper-table to explain this. Dick, anxious about her, runs lightly upstairs and looks into the room. She is sleeping a fitful, uneasy sleep. He closes the door gently and returns to Jessie.

They have supper together, and afterwards sit talking for a while; or rather Jessie talks, Dick listening and looking.

She is in one of her daring moods to-night. The end of her visit is drawing near; and, in the anticipated safety of their separation, both have grown of late, perhaps, a little reckless.

"Dick," she says suddenly, "am I looking very beautiful to-night?"

"Very beautiful," he answers, in a low tone.

"More so than usual, I mean?"

"I almost think so, for the moment."

"Take your mental picture of me now then, Dick," she cries, springing up laughing, "and destroy all the others. I want you to remember me at

---

6   As a slave in Egypt Joseph (of the 'coat of many colours') resisted seduction by Potiphar's wife but was imprisoned when she accused him of trying to seduce her. The story is told in Genesis.

my best when I am gone. Will you?"

She stands before him, looking down at him and laughing like some old-world hot-blooded goddess. Her beautiful white arms lie crossed before her, gleaming like marble in the soft lamplight. Her glorious gold-crowned head is thrown back defiantly, revealing the full, firm throat, the heaving breast beneath.

Heaven and earth rush down before Dick's eyes, and he and Jessie stand alone. He catches her in his arms. Their burning lips rush together. The room dissolves and fades. They are alone with Nature.[7]

How long a time has passed neither knows. It may have been a minute, it may have been a thousand years. Dick raises his eyes at last, and glances over Jessie's shoulder into the mirror on the mantelpiece. Then a white, speechless terror comes upon him.

The door stands open, and from the glass there looks out at him a face—a face dead, like his own.

So from that witches' mirror these two gaze at each other for a moment. Then the door softly closes to.

He says nothing to Jessie. She has seen nothing. She hurries by him without looking at him, without speaking, and passes out.

As soon as she is gone, he creeps to the stairs and listens. All is quiet. There is no light in Daisy's room. He steals back, and, taking his hat and coat, lets himself softly out of the house.

All night he walks swiftly through miles and miles of ghostly streets. Policemen flash their lanterns in his face suspiciously, coffee-stall keepers and their few customers pause in their conversation to stare after him. They say he seems like a man who has committed a crime and is trying to escape.

They have guessed nearer the truth than they really think; but the thing he is trying to escape from follows mockingly at his heels.

---

7   Originally 'their quivering limbs entwine'. Jerome made the alteration in defer-ence to Arrowsmith's concern about the likely reception of the book.

CHAPTER SIX

The Strangling of the Flowers

To escape from the returning light, more than from any other motive, he, at the first gleam of dawn, retraces his long way back to what a few hours ago he would have thought of as home.

He unlocks the door stealthily, and slinks in like a thief. The elder of the two servants, a middle-aged woman who has grown up from a slim girl in the service of Daisy's people, comes quickly forward on hearing him enter, and meets him with a grave face. She has evidently been waiting for him. Her mistress, she tells him, has passed a troubled night, and she has been growing anxious about her.

He makes some hurried explanation as to his having been called out suddenly to see a dying friend, not caring whether the woman believes him or not, and, passing her, swiftly mounts the stairs.

He opens the bedroom door softly, and looks in. Daisy has sunk into an exhausted sleep. Returning to the hall, he sends the woman for a doctor. While she is gone, he takes the opportunity to steal into the darkened room again, and bring out a change of clothes. These he takes down with him into the drawing-room, where he puts them on. Then he paces up and down, waiting.

Footsteps scrunching upon the gravel without come into the silence, and then follows a low tapping on the stained glass. He opens the hall-door, and the doctor, muffled up to the ears in a huge coat, steps inside, and, with a commonplace remark about the weather, goes up to the sick-room accompanied by the woman.

Dick hears them moving about overhead. After a while the bedroom door opens and closes, and the doctor descends.

"Oh, well, there's nothing serious," he explains to Dick. "She is terribly weak; and she has been overtaxing herself in some way or other. She *must* keep quiet. Let her stop in bed all day to-day; and as soon as you can manage it, get her away into the country."

He glances more keenly than he has done at Dick.

"You are looking seedy yourself," he adds. "A month at the seaside or in Scotland would do you both good."

He goes out, saying he will send round something to make her sleep.

Dick watches him down the road. As he steps back into the passage, he meets the servant wearing a questioning look. He tells her what the doctor has said, exaggerating somewhat the necessity for perfect quiet.

"Do not let anybody go in to her except yourself." His manner is very earnest, as if much depended upon this. "Nobody, mind; not even Miss Craig. She must not talk; she must not see anybody."

The woman promises strict observance, and he leaves the house again, explaining that he will not be home till very late. If Daisy gets worse at all, they are to send for him to the office.

All day long Dick, battling in deep waters, clutches at the flimsy hope that by some means or other he may even yet escape his punishment— that his Nemesis may, by some inducement or another, be made to rest content with shewing him the terror of her face, and come no nearer to tear him with her claws. Daisy, knowing the weakness that is upon her, may perhaps imagine—may, by the help of the cunning that desperation lends, be made to imagine—that the thing she looked upon was no reality, but some fantastic dream, some terrible creation of her own disordered brain. Nay, may it not even be—and the thought is to his mind as the gleam of a white sail to the straining eyes of a shipwrecked man—that she saw nothing, only seemed to see? There was no ray of life in the face the mirror shewed him: may it not have been the face of a sleeping person? Occasional somnambulism, he recollects, was a feature of her former illness. May not the present trouble have likewise brought this weakness in its train?

Ah, God, if it only might be so! If it had only been her senseless form that had looked through that open door, while her living, loving self had slumbered on, never to know what the dumb eyes had seen!

He dines at a restaurant, choosing the busiest one he can find. He flies from all quiet, as a haunted man from shadows. He clings to his fellow-creatures as if their presence could drive away the ghostly comrades that walk unseen beside him, looking at him with cold, dead eyes,—as if the hubbub of their careless talk could drown the silent voices ever whispering to him.

He eats little and drinks much; but the fire in his brain burns too fiercely to be quenched.

He lingers at the table till the place is nearly empty, and then hurries to a theatre. He goes into the pit.[1] There is plenty of space at each side, but in the middle the people are more closely packed. He forces his way there, and squeezes himself down between a jovial-looking, red-faced man and a couple of talkative old women. The jovial-looking man addresses occasional remarks to him from time to time. He answers with that mechanical intelligence that enables us to transact the necessities of life without really thinking, or even knowing that we are performing them. Now and again the sound of his own voice falls upon his ears and startles him, as he wanders far off, alone. The laughter of those around him breaks in upon his solitude like the laughter of children wafted on the wind to the ears of an old man. He struggles to escape from his torture-chamber of thought, to mingle with the human things that seem so near to him. He strives to watch with them the play, to take with them some interest in it. But he himself is playing in a grim comedy for the amusement of the gods. The mimicry upon the stage passes before him as a puppet show might have passed before the eyes of some doomed gladiator waiting in the arena of old Rome.

He is glad when it is over, and he can regain the quiet streets. He paces up and down them, making always for where the crowd is the densest and the glare the brightest. One by one, as public house and

1   The cheap seats directly in front of the stage. Symbolically Dick has also entered a state of infernal torment, 'the pit'.

restaurant and café close, the lights grow less, until only the street lamps are left burning. The tide of human life ebbs back into the night, leaving the streets visible. The last roysterer has disappeared. Here and there a creature of the dark lurks silently amid the shadows.[2]

He steals homeward and creeps into the house. Only a dim night-light is burning in the bedroom. He pauses outside the partly-open door and listens. From the sound of Daisy's breathing, he can tell that she is sleeping. He goes in and stands beside her. The little light shines down upon her face.

For a long time he remains there gazing at her.

Does she know? Has she seen the Truth face to face, and looked into its eyes, never to forget; or seen it, if at all, only indistinctly through a mist, as men see shapes at twilight and walk on, wondering whether they really saw or only thought they saw? Will he ever take her in his arms again; ever hear again her sweet voice calling him? or will the memory of that one moment stand ever with dividing hand between their lives?

With a groan he cries:

"Oh, God! not this punishment, but some other. I love her so!"

She turns and murmurs something. He draws back hastily, thinking she is awake; but she is only talking in her sleep.

It seems a living thing among the dead—this voice, wailing through the quiet room. Now it rises to a whispered shriek, now sinks to a low moan. He holds his breath and listens. The words escape from her unconscious lips in short, disjointed sentences:

"Yes, yes. I know. It is a dream—yes, yes, it is—a dream—a dream! Ah, let me go. Oh, don't, please don't—you will drive me mad. Ah, no! I cannot, I cannot look. —I will not—I should hate him—hate him—hate him all my life. Shut it out—don't let me see it. Don't let me see his face. Let me go—you are killing me, I tell you. Help! help!"

---

2   Jerome was always intensely aware of the divided life of the city. Significantly the respectable Dick is brought into collision with the dark side of London for the first time after his sexual fall, in this glimpse of the prostitutes standing in the shadows.

She wakes with a start, trembling in every limb. Seeing him among the shadows, she cries out, frightened:

"Dick, Dick! is that you? Am I awake?"

He moves a step or two, and stands before her. For the first time since they looked out at each other from the little gilt-framed mirror over the parlour mantelpiece, they look into each other's eyes now.

At length she speaks. Her voice is strange to him. Much of their life has passed away since he last talked with her.

"Dick, was it a dream or—the truth? Answer me, Dick. I am weak and ill. I have seen strange things. Was it a dream?"

She pauses for his reply.

The acted lie, waiting ready behind him, plucks him by the sleeve.

She leans forward in the bed. Her eyes, from which the terror has never yet died out, are close to his.

"Dick, once and for all our lives, speak—It was a dream."

He does not answer her; he does not look at her. Slowly he sinks to the floor beside her, and bows his head to the ground.

She sits staring at him for an instant; then starts back from him with a cry that rings through the silent house—that will ring long through the chambers of his brain.

The little clock upon the dressing-table ticks louder and louder till the walls of the room seem almost bursting with each throb. The night-light burns deeper and deeper into its socket, causing a thin shadow to creep upward round the room.

He rises, and brushes with his hand the dust from his clothes.

"What do you wish?" he asks quietly and a little wearily. "Shall I go away?"

"I do not know. I cannot think just now," she replies in the same fixed tone. "I must wait a little while. Leave me alone."

"Very well," he answers, and goes out, closing the door behind him.

CHAPTER SEVEN

In the Wilderness

Jessie knows nothing of what has passed between Daisy and Dick. Daisy's illness accounts to her sufficiently for all that is strange around her. She does not stop to consider very much about the thing. She has her own part in the comedy to occupy her attention.

What that part is she herself could hardly tell. All thought concerning it she has from the beginning purposely put away from her. Her luxurious nature has shrunk from the contemplation of a subject that its instinct has told it is bound to be fraught with disturbing reflections. Like a heedless child, intent only on the pleasure of the moment, she has strayed farther and farther, stretching out eager hands towards the crimson flowers. Where the path was leading her she has never paused to think.

Or if, for a moment, the thought has forced itself upon her, she has looked upward at the laughing sunshine and forward at the beckoning blossoms, and sighed to herself:

"I must turn—in a little while."

In Mrs. Grundy's select seminary for young ladies, where the dirt is carefully brushed under the mat, and rotten walls are hidden by paper of a chaste pattern, girls are warned that a certain amount of danger awaits them in life, owing to the tendency of spinsters to form unfortunate attachments with ineligible bachelors. That Nature—herself a mother—could implant in the breast of a young unmarried woman any feeling stronger than the merest friendship for somebody else's husband, Mrs. Grundy would deem too outrageously shocking an idea to be even suggested to her pupils.

To poor, carefully-brought-up Jessie, knowing human nature only as a smiling well-behaved personage of simple tastes, it has seemed that this agreeable, handsome cousin of hers was, of all men, the very one with whom to indulge in the delightful game of flirtation. He being a married man, no mistakes could arise—no harm could come to either.

So she has walked with him along the pleasant road,—somewhat farther than she had intended. For the first time she looks around, and asks herself whither she has wandered. Knowing this land of Life only by its beaten highway, she is in some doubt.

She seems to be standing in a vast desert place. It stretches before her eyes flat and grey and endless; for there is no sky above, and no horizon beyond. The pleasant road, with its yielding turf and beckoning blossoms, has vanished. The ways of life lead forward; there is no returning by them. It has led her to this pitiless land where there is no shelter and no sound of life; only silence and drifting sand.

Only one living thing is with her in this desert place—the man. She does not love him. She is not sure that she does not hate him; but she clings to the thought of him. If he leaves her, she will be alone there.

All day long she has remained in the house waiting and listening for him, dreading his coming, fearing still more his *not* coming.

Sitting in the darkness of her own room with her ear close to the partly open door, she has heard him enter and go up to Daisy's room; and a sudden fierce hate has swept over her, followed by a sudden fierce hope that grips her heart and almost stops its beating: might not Daisy die?

She smiles to herself as she reflects how the same thought would have been full of despair to her a few weeks—a few hours ago. She has left the child of yesterday very far behind her. She feels very old as she sits there listening in that dark room.

An hour or two later she hears Daisy's door open again and Dick come out, and she starts up, the hot blood rushing into her face. She hears his footsteps descend the stairs. Then she closes the door, and, throwing herself, fully dressed as she is, upon the bed, sleeps.

In the morning they meet at breakfast and speak empty commonplaces to one another that sound strange to their own ears. The situation recalls to Jessie the breakfasts of her school days with their laboured and unnaturally polite conversations in bad French, and she bursts into a choking laugh. During the meal her eyes seek his, ready to avoid them should they seek hers; but he keeps his face turned from her. How he hates her! He dare not look at her. He could hardly keep from striking her were he to do so.

He pushes his chair away and rises, and she follows him to the window.

"You are not angry with me?" she asks.

Her words, and the wistful submissiveness of her tone, sting him into a yet greater repulsion towards her, a consciousness of the injustice of which still further maddens him.

"For God's sake, don't get sentimental!" he cries, brutally. "Hate me, loathe me; anything but love me."

He has no thought for her: all his pain is for Daisy. Jessie has come between them and ruined both their lives. Does she mean to be a millstone round his neck for ever?

She stands looking at him for a while without speaking. Then suddenly glancing up into his face, she lays her hand upon his arm.

"Daisy knows?" she asks.

He does not answer.

"I'm glad of that," she says, slowly, and goes out.

Next day is the day that has long been fixed for Jessie's departure. Daisy has sent a message down that she is too ill to say good-bye to her; but as Jessie sits watching the clock in the parlour, waiting until it is time to send for her cab, the door opens, and Daisy enters, clad in a loose white robe.

A letter is in her hand; she holds it out to Jessie.

"Ann brought this up to me among mine," she says; "I wished to bring it down to you myself."

Jessie takes the letter and glances at it. It is from Barnard. She folds it up and puts it away.

"What answer do you intend to give him?"

Daisy's face is very stern beneath its pallor, and a faint, cruel smile plays round the drawn mouth.

Jessie raises her head and looks at her. There is no need for a reply. Daisy sees before her the face of a woman old before her time—of a woman who has turned over the pages of her life to the end, and read there only desolation.

The mother instinct rushes into Daisy's heart, overwhelming for the time all other thoughts. Jessie is again a shy, awkward child, in trouble (she always was in some scrape or another), and Daisy is the little woman, nearly four years older, who comforts her and tells her not to mind.

She stoops down and puts her arms about the girl.

"May God forgive him," she says, very low.

One evening, a few days later, Daisy sits in the drawing-room, cloaked and gloved. She is alone in the house, having given the two servants a holiday and told them that they need not be home till late. Six o'clock strikes. She takes her hat from a chair beside her, and crossing with it to the fireplace, puts it on by the aid of the glass above the mantelpiece. This done, she sits down again and waits.

In a little while she hears a footstep on the gravel-path, upon which she goes out into the passage, reaching it just as Dick enters. She stands watching him till he has shut the door behind him and has taken off his hat and coat, and then she steps forward.

"I have been waiting for you, Dick," she says, speaking in a quiet, even voice that is nothing but a voice, undisturbed by any throb of thought or emotion. "I am going away, and I wanted to see you and to say good-bye. I have thought it all over very carefully, and waited till I felt sure. I did not want to act rashly, or to seem to be thinking only of myself. Of course it will be a very difficult position for both of us, more so for me than for you.[1] I have considered all that. Fortunately,

---

1 Regardless of their relative faults, a woman separated from her husband was socially suspect.

there are no other lives dependent upon ours; so that only we ourselves will suffer."

She takes from the hall-table a little bag and transfers it to her left hand.

"I have arranged everything so as to keep the thing as quiet as possible," she continues. "Both the women are out. I shall walk to the station, and a cart will call to-morrow for the few things I shall need. Good-bye."

She holds out her hand.

"Do not think I have meant to be unkind, Dick. I have tried to feel differently, but I cannot. I seem to have no other feeling in me but this desire to get away. I do not know whether you can understand me; but it seems to myself as if I had been turned into stone. I do not even feel any anger against you, or any sorrow for myself. Perhaps it would be better if I did. I do not think I shall ever feel anything again."

As he makes no sign, she holds out her hand to him a second time.

"I must go now," she says. "Shall we say good-bye?"

"Good-bye," he answers dreamily, and their cold hands meet for a moment and touch. Then he opens the door for her, and she passes out, and he closes it after her.

He goes into the drawing-room, and, walking to the window, stands there with his hands in his pockets, gazing into the gathering twilight. A few drops of rain fall against the panes. He wonders if she had an umbrella with her, or if he had better try to overtake her with one.

Then suddenly the strong desire rushes upon him to go after her and cry out to her all the thoughts that are in his heart, and he starts towards the door.

Then as suddenly he checks himself.

"She would not understand!" he says; and, returning to the window, he stands watching the dead leaves whirling in the wind.

THE END

APPENDIX A

Degeneration

In an 1895 editorial in *To-Day* Jerome noted that 'A book which has recently attracted all the attention it deserves, and perhaps a little more, is the English translation of Max Nordan's [sic] work on degeneration. ... He would apply the term "degenerate" to the originators of all the *fin-de-siècle* movements in art and literature. Those who sympathize with these movements, admire the originators, and profess an exquisite appreciation that the Philistine cannot feel, are also to be considered degenerate; the appreciativeness of which they are so proud is to rank only as a disease.'

From Max Nordau, *Degeneration* (1895)
Book One: Fin de Siècle, Chapter I: The Dusk of Nations

Fin de Siècle is a name covering both what is characteristic of many modern phenomena, and also the underlying mood which in them finds expression. Experience has long shown that an idea usually derives its designation from the language of the nation which first formed it. This, indeed, is a law of constant application when historians of manners and customs inquire into language, for the purpose of obtaining some notion, through the origins of some verbal root, respecting the home of the earliest inventions and the line of evolution in different human races. *Fin-de-siècle* is French, for it was in France that the mental state so entitled was first consciously realized. The word has flown from one hemisphere to the other, and found its way into all civilized languages. A proof this that the need of it existed. The *fin-de-siècle* state of mind is to-day everywhere to be met with; nevertheless, it is in many cases a mere imitation of a foreign fashion gaining vogue, and not an organic evolution. It is in the land of its birth that it appears in its most genuine form, and Paris is the right place in which to observe its manifold expressions.

No proof is needed of the extreme silliness of the term. Only the brain of a child or of a savage could form the clumsy idea that the century is a kind of living being, born like a beast or a man, passing through all the stages of existence, gradually ageing and declining after blooming childhood, joyous youth, and vigorous maturity, to die with the expiration of the hundredth year, after being afflicted in its last decade with all the infirmities of mournful senility. Such a childish anthropomorphism or zoomorphism never stops to consider that the arbitrary division of time, rolling ever continuously along, is not identical amongst all civilized beings, and that while this nineteenth century of Christendom is held to be a creature reeling to its death presumptively in dire exhaustion, the fourteenth century of the Mahommedan world is tripping along in the baby-shoes of its first decade, and the fifteenth century of the Jews strides gallantly by in the full maturity of its fifty-second year. Every day on our globe 130,000 human beings are born, for whom the world begins with this same day, and the young citizen of the world is neither feebler nor fresher for leaping into life in the midst of the death-throes of 1900, nor on the birthday of the twentieth century. But it is a habit of the human mind to project externally its own subjective states. And it is in accordance with this naively egoistic tendency that the French ascribe their own senility to the century, and speak of *fin-de-siècle* when they ought correctly to say *fin-de-race*.[1]

---

1   This passage has been misunderstood. It has been taken to mean that all the French nation had degenerated, and their race was approaching its end. However, from the concluding paragraph of this chapter, it may be clearly seen that I had in my eye only the upper ten thousand. The peasant population, and a part of the working classes and the *bourgeoisie*, are sound. I assert only the decay of the rich inhabitants of great cities and the leading classes. It is they who have discovered *fin-de-siècle*, and it is to them also that *fin-de-race* applies. [author's original footnote]

But however silly a term *fin-de-siècle* may be, the mental constitution which it indicates is actually present in influential circles. The disposition of the times is curiously confused, a compound of feverish restlessness and blunted discouragement, of fearful presage and hang-dog renunciation. The prevalent feeling is that of imminent perdition and extinction. *Fin-de-siècle* is at once a confession and a complaint. The old Northern faith contained the fearsome doctrine of the Dusk of the Gods. In our days there have arisen in more highly-developed minds vague qualms of a Dusk of the Nations, in which all suns and all stars are gradually waning, and mankind with all its institutions and creations is perishing in the midst of a dying world.

It is not for the first time in the course of history that the horror of world-annihilation has laid hold of men's minds. A similar sentiment took possession of the Christian peoples at the approach of the year 1000. But there is an essential difference between chiliastic panic and *fin-de-siècle* excitement. The despair at the turn of the first millennium of Christian chronology proceeded from a feeling of fulness of life and joy of life. Men were aware of throbbing pulses, they were conscious of unweakened capacity for enjoyment, and found it unmitigatedly appalling to perish together with the world, when there were yet so many flagons to drain and so many lips to kiss, and when they could yet rejoice so vigorously in both love and wine. Of all this in *the fin-de-siècle* feeling there is nothing. Neither has it anything in common with the impressive twilight-melancholy of an aged Faust, surveying the work of a lifetime, and who, proud of what has been achieved, and contemplating what is begun but not completed, is seized with vehement desire to finish his work, and, awakened from sleep by haunting unrest, leaps up with the cry: 'Was ich gedacht, ich eil' es zu vollbringen.'[2]

Quite otherwise is the *fin-de-siècle* mood. It is the impotent despair of a sick man, who feels himself dying by inches in the midst of an eternally living nature blooming insolently for ever. It is the envy of a

---

2   'My thought I hasten to fulfil.' [author's original footnote]

rich, hoary voluptuary, who sees a pair of young lovers making for a sequestered forest nook; it is the mortification of the exhausted and impotent refugee from a Florentine plague, seeking in an enchanted garden the experiences of a Decamerone, but striving in vain to snatch one more pleasure of sense from the uncertain hour. The reader of Turgenieff's *A Nest of Nobles* will remember the end of that beautiful work. The hero, Lavretzky, comes as a man advanced in years to visit at the house where, in his young days, he had lived his romance of love. All is unchanged. The garden is fragrant with flowers. In the great trees the happy birds are chirping; on the fresh turf the children romp and shout. Lavretzky alone has grown old, and contemplates, in mournful exclusion, a scene where nature holds on its joyous way, caring nought that Lisa the beloved is vanished, and Lavretzky, a broken-down man, weary of life. Lavretzky's admission that, amidst all this ever-young, ever-blooming nature, for him alone there comes no morrow; Alving's dying cry for 'The sun—the sun!' in Ibsen's *Ghosts*—these express rightly the *fin-de-siècle* attitude of to-day.

This fashionable term has the necessary vagueness which fits it to convey all the half-conscious and indistinct drift of current ideas, just as the words 'freedom,' 'ideal,' 'progress' seem to express notions, but actually are only sounds, so in itself *fin-de-siècle* means nothing, and receives a varying signification according to the diverse mental horizons of those who use it.

[...]

Such is the notion underlying the word *fin-de-siècle*. It means a practical emancipation from traditional discipline, which theoretically is still in force. To the voluptuary this means unbridled lewdness, the unchaining of the beast in man; to the withered heart of the egoist, disdain of all consideration for his fellow-men, the trampling under foot of all barriers which enclose brutal greed of lucre and lust of pleasure; to the contemner of the world it means the shameless ascendency of base impulses and motives, which were, if not virtuously suppressed, at least hypocritically hidden; to the believer it means the repudiation of dogma, the negation of a super-sensuous world, the descent into flat phenomenalism; to the sensitive nature yearning for aesthetic thrills, it means the vanishing of ideals in art, and no more power in its accepted forms to arouse emotion. And to all, it means the end of an established order, which for thousands of years has satisfied logic, fettered depravity, and in every art matured something of beauty.

One epoch of history is unmistakably in its decline, and another is announcing its approach. There is a sound of rending in every tradition, and it is as though the morrow would not link itself with to-day. Things as they are totter and plunge, and they are suffered to reel and fall, because man is weary, and there is no faith that it is worth an effort to uphold them. Views that have hitherto governed minds are dead or driven hence like disenthroned kings, and for their inheritance they that hold the titles and they that would usurp are locked in struggle. Meanwhile interregnum in all its terrors prevails; there is confusion among the powers that be; the million, robbed of its leaders, knows not where to turn; the strong work their will; false prophets arise, and dominion is divided amongst those whose rod is the heavier because their time is short. Men look with longing for whatever new things are at hand, without presage whence they will come or what they will be. They have hope that in the chaos of thought, art may yield revelations of the order that is to follow on this tangled web. The poet, the musician, is to announce, or divine, or at least suggest in what forms civilization will further be evolved. What shall be considered good to-morrow—what shall be beautiful? What shall we know to-morrow—what believe in? What shall inspire us? How shall we enjoy? So rings the question from the thousand voices of the people, and where a market-vendor sets up his booth and claims to give an answer, where a fool or a knave suddenly begins to prophesy in verse or prose, in sound or colour, or professes to practise his art otherwise than his predecessors and competitors, there gathers a great concourse, crowding around him to seek in what he has wrought, as in oracles of the Pythia, some meaning to be divined and interpreted.

And the more vague and insignificant they are, the more they seem to convey of the future to the poor gaping souls gasping for revelations, and the more greedily and passionately are they expounded.

Such is the spectacle presented by the doings of men in the reddened light of the Dusk of the Nations. Massed in the sky the clouds are aflame in the weirdly beautiful glow which was observed for the space of years after the eruption of Krakatoa. Over the earth the shadows creep with deepening gloom, wrapping all objects in a mysterious dimness, in which all certainty is destroyed and any guess seems plausible. Forms lose their outlines, and are dissolved in floating mist. The day is over, the night draws on. The old anxiously watch its approach, fearing they will not live to see the end. A few amongst the young and strong are conscious of the vigour of life in all their veins and nerves, and rejoice in the coming sunrise. Dreams, which fill up the hours of darkness till the breaking of the new day, bring to the former comfortless memories, to the latter high-souled hopes. And in the artistic products of the age we see the form in which these dreams become sensible.

Here is the place to forestall a possible misunderstanding.

The great majority of the middle and lower classes is naturally not *fin-de-siècle*. It is true that the spirit of the times is stirring the nations down to their lowest depths, and awaking even in the most inchoate and rudimentary human being a wondrous feeling of stir and upheaval. But this more or less slight touch of moral sea-sickness does not excite in him the cravings of travailing women, nor express itself in new aesthetic needs. The Philistine or the Proletarian still finds undiluted satisfaction in the old and oldest forms of art and poetry, if he knows himself unwatched by the scornful eye of the votary of fashion, and is free to yield to his own inclinations. He prefers Ohnet's novels to all the symbolists, and Mascagni's *Cavalleria Rusticana* to all Wagnerians and to Wagner himself; he enjoys himself royally over slap-dash farces and music-hall melodies, and yawns or is angered at Ibsen; he contemplates gladly chromos of paintings depicting Munich beer-houses and rustic taverns, and passes the open-air painters without a glance. It is only a very small minority who honestly find pleasure in the new tendencies, and announce them with genuine conviction as that which alone is sound, a sure guide for the future, a pledge of pleasure and of moral benefit. But this minority has the gift of covering the whole visible surface of society, as a little oil extends over a large area of the surface of the sea. It consists chiefly of rich educated people, or of fanatics. The former give the *ton* to all the snobs, the fools, and the blockheads; the latter make an impression upon the weak and dependent, and intimidate the nervous. All snobs affect to have the same taste as the select and exclusive minority, who pass by everything that once was considered beautiful with an air of the greatest contempt. And thus it appears as if the whole of civilized humanity were converted to the aesthetics of the Dusk of the Nations.

APPENDIX B

Novel Notes

Serialised in *The Idler* between May 1892 and April 1893, *Novel Notes* is almost exactly contemporaneous with *Weeds* and several of its sketches share the novella's theme of sexual corruption.

As a rule one is the hero of one's own dreams,[1] but at times I have dreamt a dream entirely in the third person—a dream with the incidents of which I have had no connection whatever, except as an unseen and impotent spectator. One of these I have often thought about since, wondering if it could not be worked up into a story. But perhaps it would be too painful a theme.

I dreamt I saw a woman's face among a throng. It is an evil face, but there is a strange beauty in it. I see it come and go, moving in and out among the shadows. The flickering gleams thrown by street lamps flash down upon it, showing the wonder of its evil fairness. Then the lights go out.

I see it next in a place that is very far away, and it is even more beautiful than before, for the evil has gone out of it. Another face is looking down into it, a bright, pure face. The faces meet and kiss, and, as his lips touch hers, the blood mounts to her cheeks and brow. I see the two faces again. But I cannot tell where they are or how long a time has passed. The man's face has grown a little older, but it is still young and fair, and when the woman's eyes rest upon it there comes a glory into her face, so that it is like the face of an angel. But at times

---

1 Quite possibly an allusion to David Copperfield, who memorably turns out to be the hero of his own life.

the woman is alone, and then I see the old evil look struggling back.

Then I see clearer. I see the room in which they live. It is very poor. An old-fashioned piano stands in one corner, and beside it is a table on which lie scattered a tumbled mass of papers round an inkstand. An empty chair waits before the table. The woman sits by the open window.

She seems to be sitting there for a long while. From far below there rises the sound of a great city. Its lights throw up faint beams into the dark room. The smell of its streets is in the woman's nostrils.

Every now and again she looks toward the door and listens, then turns to the open window. And I notice that each time she looks toward the door the evil in her face shrinks back; but each time she turns to the window it grows more fierce and sullen.

Suddenly she starts up, and there is a terror in her eyes that frightens me as I dream, and I see great beads of sweat upon her brow. Then, very slowly, her face changes, and I see again the evil creature of the night. She wraps around her an old cloak, and creeps out. I hear her footsteps going down the stairs. They grow fainter and fainter. I hear a door open. The roar of the streets rushes up into the house, and the woman's footsteps are swallowed up.

Time drifts onward through my dream. Scenes change, take shape, and fade; but all is vague and undefined, until, out of the dimness, there fashions itself a long, deserted street. The lights make glistening circles on the wet pavement. A figure, dressed in gaudy rags, slinks by, keeping close against the wall. Its back is toward me, and I do not see its face. Another figure glides from out the shadows. I look upon its face, and I see it is the face that the woman's eyes gazed up into and worshiped long ago when my dream was just begun. But the fairness and the purity are gone from it, and it is old and evil, as the woman's when I looked upon her last. The figure in the gaudy rags moves slowly on. The second figure follows it, and overtakes it. The two pause, and speak to one another as they draw near. The street is very dark where they have met, and the figure in the gaudy rags keeps its face still turned aside. They walk on together, side by side, in silence, till they come to where a flaring gas-lamp hangs before a tavern; and there the woman turns, and I see that it is the woman of my dream. And she and the man look into each other's eyes once more.

APPENDIX C

Ella Hepworth Dixon

As an identifiable New Woman, Ella Hepworth Dixon represented a figure persistently attacked by Jerome in the 1890s. In 1895 she contributed to a satirical (on both sides) debate in *The Idler*, 'How to court the "Advanced Woman"'. Idlers' Club. *The Idler* 6 (August 1894 - January 1895): 192-211.

Ella Hepworth Dixon, 'Why Women are Ceasing to Marry' (1899)

This question has been so often discussed from the strictly utilitarian aspect, that one may be pardoned for taking what, at the first blush, might be considered a somewhat flippant view of an alarming social phenomenon. It has been seriously argued—generally by masculine writers and elderly ladies who find themselves out of sympathy with the modern feminist movement—that women, nowadays, are disposed, from selfish reasons, to shirk the high privileges and duties of maternity and domestic life, to wish to compete with men, and undersell the market from motives of pure vanity, and to have so far unsexed themselves as to have lost the primordial instinct for conjugal life altogether.

Now, that any of these propositions are true can be denied by anyone even superficially acquainted with the modern movement, with those who lead it and with those who follow it. I forget which distinguished writer has said that 'every woman, in her heart, hankers after a linen-cupboard,' and this delightful aphorism may be truthfully applied, I take it, to every kind of modern woman, except the gypsy class of globe-trotters.

No. The reason why women are ceasing to marry must rather be attributed to a shifting feminine point of view, to a more critical attitude towards their masculine contemporaries. If, of late, they would seem to have shown a disposition to avoid the joys, cares, and responsibilities of the linen-cupboard, it is chiefly. I think, because their sense of humour is often as keen as it was once supposed to be blunted. The proper adoring feminine attitude does not, it would seem, come naturally to the present generation, who are apt not so much—in Miltonic phrase—to 'see God' in their average suitors as to perceive in these young gentlemen certain of the least endearing qualities of the Anglo-Saxon race; those qualities, it may be whispered, which, though eminently suitable for the making of Empire, are not always entirely appreciated on the domestic hearth.[1] This critical attitude among the womenfolk is no doubt mostly due to the enormous strides which have been made in feminine education during the last twenty years, though I hasten to add that that education has made them far more tolerant and broadminded, so that the average of domestic felicity will undoubtedly be higher as things progress. Indeed, the famous phrase, 'Tout comprendre, c'est tout pardonner,'[2] is most applicable of all to the eternal question of the sexes, and the man or woman who has mastered its significance is well on the way to make an ideal partner in marriage.

At present, however, we are in a transition stage,[3] and there is a certain amount of misunderstanding nowadays between the sexes which make marrying and giving in marriage a somewhat hazardous enterprise.

This new and critical attitude on the part of the fair is a thing of quite recent growth. Before, and up to as late as, the mid-Victorian

---

1 Dixon critiques changing gender roles, questioning the suitability of the masculine ideal as presented by adventure writers such as Rider Haggard, for the domestic relations in which men actually stand to women.

2 To understand all is to forgive all

3 A view shared by Mona Caird and other feminists of the period.

era, the recognised wifely pose was one of blind adoration. Directly a girl married she was supposed to think her husband perfect, unapproachable, wise and beautiful beyond all measure, and of a stupendous understanding. Most of the married ladies in the great mid-Victorian novels looked up to their spouses with admiration tempered by awe. Now that we have educated our womenfolk into a sense of humour—and there is no surer test of breadth of mind—this wifely meekness is no longer possible. Yet, seeing how the old masculine idols are shattered, and the heroes of ladies' novels are no longer Greek gods, or Guardsmen,[4] or even men of blameless life, it is impossible not to sympathise with our masculine contemporaries, *Ces Rois en Exile*,[5] who have lost a crown, and who have not yet made up their minds to swear 'Liberty, Equality, Fraternity!'[6] with their feminine critics. It is possible, moreover, that the modern man has begun to see the humorous side of the question also. Occasionally he shows a disposition to step down from his pedestal, and even to mix, on equal terms, with his more enlightened feminine friends. No less a modern person, for instance, than Mr. William Archer,[7] has publicly stated that he cannot sit in his stall at the theatre and listen to Katherine's abject speech about 'her lord, her king, her governor,' at the end of 'The Taming of the Shrew.'

> *Then vail your stomachs, for it is no boot;*
> *And place your hands below your husband's foot;*
> *In token of which duty, if he please,*
> *My hand is ready, may it do him ease.'*

---

4 Such as are found in the society novels of Ouida, a notable anti-feminist writer.

5 Those kings in exile.

6 Dixon humorously compares the 'anarchic' New Woman to the French revolutionaries of the late eighteenth century.

7 William Archer (1856-1924) was a Scottish critic, dramatist and translator, most notable for introducing Ibsen to the English stage. His work with New Woman writer Elizabeth Robins would have endeared him to Dixon.

This was the old idea of marriage. It will be readily seen that we have changed our ideals, and that if it is somewhat of an exaggeration to say that 'women are ceasing to marry,' it is certain that indiscriminate marrying has, to a certain extent, gone out. In short, *le premier venu*[8] in no longer the successful wooer that he once was. Then, too, this shyness at being caught in the matrimonial net is largely a characteristic of the modern English maiden, for widows, like widowers, usually show an extraordinary eagerness to resume the fetters of the wedded state. Some recent amusing statistics on this subject proved that a man of forty remains a widower for two years only, while his feminine prototype shows even greater eagerness to console herself, for, under the age of thirty-five, she marries again within twenty months.

But we are at present concerned with bachelors and spinsters, of persons, in short, who have still the great experiment to make. It is certain that marriage—and its attendant responsibilities, the bringing up and starting in life of children—is looked upon far more seriously than our immediate forbears were wont to regard it. Elizabeth Barrett Browning (who, as the author of 'Aurora Leigh' undoubtedly proclaimed herself one of the earliest of the 'new women')[9] was mortally afraid of marriage and did not attempt to conceal the fact from her adoring lover. In her recently published letters to Robert Browning, it is amusing to see how—just like any modern woman of 1899—she constantly threatens, that if they do not 'get on' when they are married, she will leave him and go to Greece. This question of 'going to Greece' becomes one of their principal humorous efforts, but there is just an acid flavour about it that makes one a little doubtful whether the distinguished author of 'Pippa Passes' appreciated the lady's constant references to such a contingency. In short, the invalid poetess who had lain for five years on a sofa, and whose knowledge of life must have been largely intuitive, was, in 1846, as timorous of

8 The first comer.

9 This perceived link with an earlier generation of women writers is in line with Dixon's commitment to a feminist discourse of community between women.

entering on the adventure of marriage as the heroine of a modern problem novel.

The author of the 'Sonnets from the Portuguese' was probably alone in her generation. Then, indeed, was the happy-go-lucky time of Dan Cupid. A strictly brought-up young person was not supposed to have the only woman's privilege , the privilege of saying 'No.' She married, as a matter of course, the first young man who offered to settle down, pay taxes, and raise a family, and that family, unfortunately for her, sometimes assumed alarming proportions.[10] This middle-class recklessness has brought, in this generation, its own Nemesis: an enormous number of young men who are obliged to seek a living in India, Africa, Canada, Australia and New Zealand; a still larger number of young women who have to stay at home and partly earn their own livelihood.

It is in this way that we have got our young people not only separated by oceans and continents, but curiously afraid of making an experiment which their fathers and mothers entered upon—like the French in the war of 1870—with a light heart. The young girl of to-day, again, has read her 'Doll's House,' and is, it may be, firmly resolved to play the part of Nora in the conjugal duologue, and to refuse, in the now classic phrase, to be any man's 'squirrel.'[11] On his side, the modern young man shows a shrewd tendency to acquire in his wife not so much one of these engaging zoological specimens as a young person who will be able to pay the weekly bills and help him substantially in his career.

All these things, naturally, make for circumspection in marriage, and there are other reasons, chiefly owing to the amazing changes in the social life of women which have gradually come about during recent years. Someone has boldly laid it down that it is the bicycle which has finally emancipated women, but it is certain that there are other factors besides the useful and agreeable wheel.

---

10 Dixon would have been aware of the widespread use of birth control among her own generation.

11 Ibsen's plays were still controversial at this time.

For it is, primarily, the almost complete downfall of Mrs. Grundy that makes the modern spinster's lot, in many respects, an eminently attractive one. Formerly, girls married in order to gain their social liberty; now, they more often remain single to bring about that desirable consummation. If young and pleasing women are permitted by public opinion to go to college, to live alone, to travel, to have a profession, to belong to a club, to give parties, to read and discuss whatever seems good to them, and to go to theatres without masculine escort, they have most of the privileges—and several others thrown in—for which the girl twenty or thirty years ago was ready to barter herself to the first suitor who offered himself and the shelter of his name. Then, again, a capable woman who has begun a career and feels certain of advancement in it, is often as shy of entangling herself matrimonially as ambitious young men have ever shown themselves under like circumstances. Indeed, the disadvantages of marriage to a woman with a profession are more obvious than to a man, and it is just this question of maternity, with all its duties and responsibilities, which is, no doubt, occasionally the cause of many women forswearing the privileges of the married state. To be quite candid, however, I think this is very seldom the real cause of a girl's remaining single. Once her affections are involved, that bundle of nerves and emotions which we call woman is often capable of all the heroisms, and who has not numbered among their friends some delicate creature—the case of Mrs. Oliphant is one in point—who has not only supported, by her own exertions, the children she bore, but the father of those children?

The modern woman, to be sure, is capable of supporting the father of her children, if she happens to be fond of that especial individual, but not (to put an extreme case) of marrying that father in order to regularise an anomalous position. The most successful German play of recent times treats, indeed, of this very subject. Herr Suderman's Magda, tyrannised over at home, goes out into the wide world and becomes a famous actress. Meanwhile, during her Wanderjahre, she has had a lover, a priggish young man whom she has met in Berlin.

Their relations were soon broken off, and the lover is not even aware that the beautiful young actress has had a child. On her return home, years after, she meets this man again, and he offers her marriage, providing their former *liaison* is kept secret, and the child kept away. Magda indignantly refuses, and goes back to her art, taking her little girl openly with her. The fact of her maternity, she holds, has ennobled her; her marriage with a hypocrite and a coward would degrade her in her own eyes.

This, it is true, may be described as the ultra-modern view of marriage and all that it entails, and it is one which obtains support only among the Teutonic races. The theory that a wedding ceremony mended all and ended all, is one which thoughtful Northern and Western peoples are nowadays inclined to dispute. Formerly, if there were a breath of scandal—sometimes totally unfounded—about two young people, well, you sent for the parson, rung the church-bells, and let the young couple make the best of this rash mating. Whether they were happy or not ever after, sad or merry, prosperous or unfortunate, was no affair of their neighbours. They were married; they had been sacrificed to society's rigorous demand for the outward observance of the proprieties; and if they chafed and fumed, or, finding themselves totally unsuited to each other, broke their spirits or their hearts, why so did other excellent citizens, people whom Robert Louis Stevenson quaintly calls 'respectable married people, with umbrellas,'[12] who had bound themselves with the same well-nigh indissoluble bonds.

It is just this general doubt of the institution of marriage, joined to that higher ideal of the wedded state with which most educated women seem to be imbued, that makes many people pause on the brink, and, choosing the known evil, remain celibate rather than fly to others that they know not of. It is possible, indeed, that a single woman of altruistic tendencies may argue that, if she is unhappy single, only one person suffers; whereas, if she should marry, and the union turn out disagreeable, probably two people will be made miserable, and, in

---

12 'Aes Triplex' 1878

all probability—several people more.

Possibly it was better for the race (if quantity, and not quality, go to the making of a nation) when its feminine half was troubled by no such doubts, but married herself on the faintest provocation, and had no misgivings at rearing a numerous progeny. On the other hand, it would seem certain that if woman continues to cultivate her critical faculties and her sense of humour—to exercise, in short, her feminine prerogative of deliberate choice in the great affair of matrimony—that the standard of human felicity will be steadily raised, and the wedded state will shine forth in a different light to that in which it stands revealed to many thoughtful persons to-day.

In that golden age, indeed, when the equality of the sexes is reached, it is probable that the shrew, the nagging woman, and the jealous wife will all have become curious specimens of a by-gone era. When a man marries, in short, it is to be hoped that he will no longer 'domesticate the "Recording Angel,"'[13] but will welcome to his hearth an agreeable companion, a gracious mistress, and a loyal friend.

---

13 R. L. Stevenson, 'Virginus Puerisque' 1881.

APPENDIX D

Mona Caird

Jerome repeatedly attacked Caird in articles of the 1880s and '90s. In response to her famous article on 'Marriage' in the *Westminster Review* in August 1888, he suggested with mock weariness that 'we all give it up, and play at something else'. Nonetheless Caird, like Dixon, contributed to *The Idler* and Jerome approved of her anti-vivisection stance rather more than her feminist polemic.

Does Marriage Hinder a Woman's Self-development?

Perhaps it might throw some light on the question whether marriage interferes with a woman's self development and career, if we were to ask ourselves honestly how a man would fare in the position, say, of his own wife.

We will take a mild case, so as to avoid all risk of exaggeration.

Our hero's wife is very kind to him. Many of his friends have far sadder tales to tell. Mrs. Brown is fond of her home and family. She pats the children on the head when they come down to dessert, and plies them with chocolate creams, much to the detriment of their health; but it amuses Mrs. Brown. Mr. Brown superintends the bilious attacks, which the lady attributes to other causes. As she never finds fault with the children, and generally remonstrates with their father, in a good-natured way, when *he* does so, they are devoted to the indulgent parent, and are inclined to regard the other as second-rate.

Meal-times are often trying in this household, for Sophia is very particular about her food; sometimes she sends it out with a rude message to the cook. Not that John objects to this. He wishes she would do it oftener, for the cook gets used to Mr. Brown's second-hand version of his wife's language. He simply cannot bring himself to hint at Mrs. Brown's robust objurgations. She *can* express herself when it comes to a question of her creature comforts!

John's faded cheeks, the hollow lines under the eyes, and hair out of curl, speak of the struggle for existence as it penetrates to the fireside. If Sophia but knew what it meant to keep going the multitudinous details and departments of a household! Her idea of adding housemaids and pageboys whenever there is a jolt in the machinery has landed them in expensive disasters, time out of mind. And then, it hopelessly cuts off all margin of income for every other purpose. It is all rather discouraging for the hero of this petty, yet gigantic tussle, for he works, so to speak, in a hostile camp, with no sympathy from his entirely unconscious spouse, whom popular sentiment nevertheless regards as the gallant protector of his manly weakness.

If incessant vigilance, tact, firmness, foresight, initiative, courage and judgment—in short, all the qualities required for governing a kingdom, and more—have made things go smoothly, the wife takes it as a matter of course; if they go wrong, she naturally lays the blame on the husband. In the same way, if the children are a credit to their parents, that is only as it should be. But if they are naughty, and fretful, and stupid, and untidy, is it not clear that there must be some serious flaw in the system which could produce such results in the offspring of Mrs. Brown? What word in the English language is too severe to describe the man who neglects to watch with sufficient vigilance over his children's health and moral training, who fails to see that his little boys' sailor-suits and knickerbockers are in good repair, that their boot lace ends do not fly out from their ankles at every step, that their hair is not like a hearth-brush, that they do not come down to dinner every day with dirty hands?

To every true man, the cares of fatherhood and home are sacred and all-sufficing. He realises, as he looks around at his little ones, that they are his crown and recompense.

John often finds that *his* crown-and-recompense gives him a racking headache by war-whoops and stampedes of infinite variety, and there are moments when he wonders in dismay if he is really a true man! He has had the privilege of rearing and training five small crowns and recompenses, and he feels that he could face the future if further privilege, of this sort, were denied him. Not but that he is devoted to his family. Nobody who understands the sacrifices he has made for them could doubt that. Only, he feels that those parts of his nature which are said to distinguish the human from the animal kingdom are getting rather effaced.

He remembers the days before his marriage, when he was so bold, in his ignorant youth, as to cherish a passion for scientific research. He even went so far as to make a chemical laboratory of the family box-room, till attention was drawn to the circumstance by a series of terrific explosions, which shaved off his eyebrows, blackened his scientific countenance, and caused him to be turned out, neck and crop, with his crucibles, and a sermon on the duty that lay nearest him,—which resolved itself into that of paying innumerable afternoon calls with his father and brothers, on acquaintances selected—as he declared in his haste—for their phenomenal stupidity. His father pointed out how selfish it was for a young fellow to indulge his own little fads and fancies, when he might make himself useful in a nice manly way, at home.

When, a year later, the scapegrace Josephine, who had caused infinite trouble and expense to all belonging to her, showed a languid interest in chemistry, a spare room was at once fitted up for her, and an extraordinary wealth of crucibles provided by her delighted parents; and when explosions and smells pervaded the house, her father, with a proud smile, would exclaim: "What genius and enthusiasm that dear girl does display!" Josephine afterwards became a distinguished professor, with an awestruck family, and a husband who made it his chief duty and privilege to save her from all worry and interruption in her valuable work.

John, who knows in his heart of hearts that he could have walked round Josephine, in the old days, now speaks with manly pride of his sister, the Professor. His own bent, however, has always been so painfully strong that he even yet tries to snatch spare moments for his researches; but the strain in so many directions has broken down his health. People always told him that a man's constitution was not fitted for severe brain-work. He supposes it is true.

During those odd moments, he made a discovery that seemed to him of value, and he told Sophia about it, in a mood of scientific enthusiasm. But she burst out laughing, and said he would really be setting the Thames on fire if he didn't take care.

"Perhaps you will excuse my remarking, my dear, that I think you might be more usefully, not to say becomingly employed, in attending to your children and your household duties, than in dealing with explosive substances in the back dining-room."

And Sophia tossed off her glass of port in such an unanswerable manner, that John felt as if a defensive reply would be almost of the nature of a sacrilege. So he remained silent, feeling vaguely guilty. And as Johnny took measles just then, and it ran through the house, there was no chance of completing his work, or of making it of public value.

Curiously enough, a little later, Josephine made the very same discovery—only rather less perfect—and every one said, with acclamation, that science had been revolutionised by a discovery before which that of gravitation paled.

John still hoped, after twenty years of experience, that presently, by some different arrangement, some better management on his part, he would achieve leisure and mental repose to do the work that his heart was in; but that time never came.

No doubt John was not infallible, and made mistakes in dealing with his various problems: do the best of us achieve consummate wisdom? No doubt, if he had followed the advice that we could all have supplied him with, in such large quantities, he might have done rather more than he did. But the question is: Did his marriage interfere with his self-development and career, and would many other Johns, in his circumstances, have succeeded much better?

Victorian Secrets

Below the Fairy City: A Life of Jerome K. Jerome
by Carolyn W. de la L. Oulton

Jerome K. Jerome (1859-1927) was the author of *Three Men in a Boat*, one of the best-loved books in the English language, but much of his prolific career has been left unexplored. Over a period of forty years, Jerome was variously a humourist, novelist, journalist, essayist and dramatist, leaving behind him a prodigious quantity of work, belying his famous quote "I like work. It fascinates me. I could sit and look at it for hours."

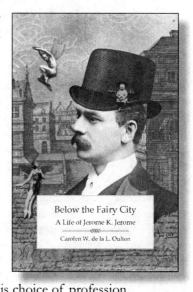

Below the Fairy City

A Life of Jerome K. Jerome

Carolyn W. de la L. Oulton

In this major new biography, Carolyn Oulton unearths hitherto unknown details of Jerome's early life in Walsall with his Micawberish father and God-fearing mother, and follows his momentous move to the Fairy City of London, where a formative encounter with Charles Dickens influenced his choice of profession.

Although famous for his unerring ability to capture middle-class experience in comic form, Oulton also reveals Jerome's serious side as campaigner on animal rights, champion of the underdog, and fierce opponent of the New Woman. Jerome was desperate to shake off the persistent association with larking about on the Thames, but never quite achieved it in his own lifetime.

Jerome K. Jerome is revealed in Oulton's book as a complex figure worthy of reassessment, with his contradictions, idiosyncrasies and, above all, his exquisite wit.

ISBN: 978-1-906469-37-5

Available in paperback, Kindle and EPUB editions.

www.victoriansecrets.co.uk

Victorian Secrets

Vice Versa, Or A Lesson to Fathers
by F. Anstey

edited with an introduction and notes
by Peter Merchant

First published in 1882, *Vice Versâ* shows the disastrous consequences of having one's wishes granted. After delivering a pompous lecture to his son Dick, stuffy Paul Bultitude declares his wish to be a schoolboy once more so he can enjoy the carefree existence of youth. Unfortunately for him, he happens to be clutching the mysterious and magical Garudâ stone, and suddenly finds himself transformed into the diminutive body of his son. Dick quickly uses the stone to his own advantage, assuming his father's portly character and swapping roles. While Dick gets the opportunity to run his father's business in the City and wreak havoc on the household, Paul must endure the privations of the brutal boarding school he forced young Dick to attend. Determined not to lose his dignity, Paul retains his former bombastic demeanour, leading to a series of hilarious episodes with the cane-wielding Dr Grimstone.

F. ANSTEY
Vice Versâ
edited by Peter Merchant

This new scholarly edition includes a critical introduction by Peter Merchant, author biography, explanatory footnotes, and a wealth of contextual material.

Available in paperback, Kindle and EPUB editions.

ISBN: 978-1-906469-21-4

www.victoriansecrets.co.uk

Lightning Source UK Ltd.
Milton Keynes UK
UKOW052240271112

202852UK00016B/1048/P

Motor launches continued to operate from Dover after the liberation of the French Channel ports, including this ML300 seen here with her crew swabbing the decks. On the forecastle are seamen 'Willie' Gillie, John 'Lofty' Gibbon, Joe Miller, and Granville Hetherall with the water hose. Alongside is a motor gunboat with 20 mm Q/F gun, smoke pots, depth charges and a float for their minesweeping paravane (bottom right).

These salvaged German helmets were found floating in Calais harbour upon the crew's arrival at the port. 'I'm the one on the left on the wheelhouse roof in the white Jersey', noted A.B. Burgess on the back of this photo which he sent to his wife. Both Calais and Boulogne were hurriedly evacuated by the Germans before capture, leaving equipment and uniforms behind for locals to liberate.